9 MM

Mike Gomes

Published by Mike Gomes, 2017.

9 MM

First edition. October 5, 2017.

ISBN: 978-1977609946

Written by Mike Gomes.

Chapter 1

———

Pulling the door open he reached up with his free hand and fixed his wind-tousled hair. The sound of raucous chatter and glasses clinking together filled the air. Surveying the bar, he shook off the cold and looked for a booth to sit at.

The bar was alive with action despite the early hour of 4:00pm, but just like so many college towns, Thursday night is a going out night, and the students of Tridon college were of a like mind.

The handsome young man had the look of any boy-next-door; short cropped hair he would let get a little longer on top, and a smooth and clear complexion that sat well with his strong yet modestly developed body.

In his hand he held a single yellow rose and he placed it on the edge of the first table he found open. Pulling out his phone he opened the applications and found 'Hooked', an app that promoted itself as a dating aid, but was more widely known for its use in finding one-night-stands for college kids and those in their 20's.

Scrolling through the endless list of women on the prowl he filtered his search down to his local area and pulled up the in-app locator showing how many women were within one mile of his present location. The stats bar zipped across the top of his phone as the page loaded and revealed eight women who were ready to mingle. Two had added pictures to their profile.

Brave, or stupid? he thought, looking over the two women and deciding to send an instant message to the one on the right, a cute girl with straight black hair and a slightly wild look in her eye.

Within moments of hitting 'Send' a message came back. "Do I know you?" she asked.

"No. Just saw your picture and wondered if you would like to meet for a drink."

"I don't even know you."

The young man smiled to himself and thought, *why do women need to play this game of cat and mouse. She knows why she's on the app and I know why she's on the app. No need to pretend we aren't on the same page.*

But he continued to play the game and build a virtual relationship with the girl, like he had done so many times before, until finally the young man was ready to make his move.

"Well, if you're uncomfortable meeting someone new I can understand that. Take care." He hit send and waited, without taking his eyes from his phone. He smiled, waiting for what he knew was soon going to come.

BING!

Incoming message. "What bar are you at? How will I know who you are?"

Fifteen minutes later the door opened again, and the young woman from the photo entered looking for the man with the yellow rose. Walking over to the table she picked up the rose and smelled it.

"Is this for me?"

"It always has been," replied the charming young man, smiling. "Please, have a seat so we can talk."

The woman slid into the seat across from him and pulled off her coat. "I don't usually meet guys on Hooked. It was my first time."

"I'm kind of a rookie myself. What's your name?"

"Cassandra."

"Beautiful name to go with a beautiful girl."

"Ha. Does that line ever work for you?" she jabbed.

He smiled again. "I hope it works now. Besides... it's true."

The couple talked for another hour while consuming several drinks during the conversation. Again and again he ordered tequila shooters, a favorite among the local college kids. As her body started to sway to the beat of the tequila, her inhabitations swayed too and she slid across onto the same side of the booth.

"You're real cute," she slurred, running her hand clumsily through his hair.

"So are you," he replied, leaning in to give her a soft kiss that she greeted with more intensity than he expected.

"Let's go back to your place and you can show me around," she suggested.

"I live kind of far away but there is a hotel right around the corner. Maybe I can show you around there instead."

"I don't care if it's the back of your car at this point," she said, taking him by the hand and moving for the door.

Spilling out onto the street the two young lovers embraced for another kiss and started to hustle their way up the street aiming directly for the door of Hotel Dowdy.

Stopping in her tracks Cassandra attempted to compose herself. "Do you have a condom? I don't need to get pregnant my first year in college."

"Yes, I have a condom. I'm sure you'll be fine."

Entering the reception, the man checked in at the front desk as Cassandra slumped down on the couch.

"Is the young lady okay?" questioned the bellhop.

"Ya. She just had a little too much to drink tonight. No bags, but thanks," replied the man, placing a $50 bill into the hand of the bellhop.

"Thank you, Sir,"

Corralling her into the elevator and then out again on the fifth floor, he slipped the pass card through the strip on the door of room 504, opening it into a generic hotel room with a queen size bed.

Cassandra staggered in and flipped on the light.

"Wooooo" she called out, sitting on the edge of the bed then bouncing up and down. "This is what we're here for. Time to party."

"Oh, it's going to be a party. Wait 'till you see what I can do."

Cassandra smiled and started pulling her arms from her shirt, revealing her bra for her new partner to see. Sitting on the edge of the bed, she stared up at him as he took a step closer. Her index finger went to the corner of her mouth in an attempt to be sexy, but it simply showed how intoxicated she was.

"Do you like what you see?" she asked. "Do you want what you see?"

"Yes."

"Say please. Ask me nicely and I'll let you have some."

"I don't beg," he replied firmly, the expression on his face hardening. "I take what I want."

Reaching down he placed his hands under her arms and pulled her up close to him. She let out a gasp of excitement at him taking charge of the situation. Leaning in he kissed her hard, ripping the bra from her body and scratching down her back.

"Oooowwwww!" she yelled as his nails dug into her back. "Not so rough."

"Shut the fuck up! You belong to me!" he barked, striking her in the face with a closed fist that knocked her back onto the bed.

Sobbing, Cassandra yelled out in pain and fear as blood started running from the corner of her eye and nose.

"I told you to shut up!" demanded the man, jumping onto the bed and punching her in the face again. As she groaned in pain he grabbed the sheet and stuffed the corner of it into her mouth to gag her. Grabbing her face between his thumb and index finger he pulled her face to within inches of his. "I told you that you belong to me. You are my property. Now time to shut up!"

Cassandra's eyes widened and she fell silent, fearing the young man with the cold blue eyes.

"That's better," he said. "Don't worry. I'm not going to rape you. I'm not a rapist. I have better plans for us. Don't fight me, or things could get very, very bad for you. Do you understand?"

Cassandra nodded, keeping her focus on the madman despite her swelling black eye.

His hands worked quickly, removing all the clothing from the woman's body and leaving her nude and crying on the bed with the sheet still stuffed in her mouth. He stood at the edge of the bed to examine his handy work, his breaths now coming quicker.

"Now is the time. Yes, now," he said under his breath while feeling himself through his pants.

Climbing back onto the bed he knelt beside the woman and looked down into her tear-filled eyes.

"I think if you just let go you will enjoy this as much as I will. It's an amazing experience."

The woman looked up in horror as the young man climbed on top of her, fully clothed, and started to rub against her. Grinding his body hard against hers he started to groan and his fingers dug hard into her arms, causing her to squeal in pain.

Pushing himself up onto his hands he looked down into her terrified eyes.

"You're not happy?" he questioned with frustration. "You're so ungrateful."

Ramming his head down hard he cracked her nose in three places and broke her cheekbone, causing the sheet to flail from her mouth. A loud moan emanated from deep within her battered body.

"Oh ya, that's what I like," he muttered as his hands found their way up to her neck. Applying only slight pressure he could feel he was just lightly cutting off her air. He slid his face close to hers.

"This is the best part. Better than any orgasm you could ever have. Just enjoy it."

Cassandra's hands flailed, trying to strike at the man and wrench his hands away from her neck. The more she struggled the more he moaned in excitement.

Grinding his hips harder into her he tightened his grip and felt her gasping. Her arms were losing strength and her blows had no effect at all.

"That's a good girl," he whispered. "Give it to me. Give me your death. Right into my hands. Give it to me."

Squeezing just a little harder he eliminated all hope for any air reaching her lungs or blood getting to her brain. Cassandra's body started to quiver, then lash out on nothing more than reflex.

"You're dying," slipped from his mouth as her heart finally stopped beating. Still laying on top of her and covered in sweat, the young man attempted to catch his breath.

Leaning over to the woman he had just killed he kissed her cheek. "Thank you," he whispered.

Rolling to the side of the bed he pulled himself into the chair next to the window so he could look back over at the body. A smile crossed his face.

Boom!

The door of the room crashed open to reveal three police officers rushing in with their weapons drawn.

"Don't move or I will shoot!" yelled one of the officers, his eyes darting between the man and the body on the bed.

Just outside the door a woman in a bathrobe was pointing to the door while speaking with two other officers, telling them where the screaming was coming from.

Without hesitation, the police threw the man to the floor, then handcuffed him.

"You're going to jail you sick bastard."

"You must not know my dad," replied the young man, his face pressed firmly against the floor. He was smiling.

Chapter 2

S tubbing out the cigarette into an ashtray Falau let out a sigh.

"I am sorry, Sir, but we have a strict policy of no smoking in the diner," said the young manager with pimples on his face.

"Ya, ya. Sorry. I forgot."

"I hope this will not cause you to look for another place for your meal."

"No. Don't worry about it," said the big man with a dismissive flip of his hand to the younger guy, who was no more than eight years his junior though it felt there was a lifetime between them.

Falau was dressed in a flannel shirt and a beat-up pair of jeans. His old tennis shoes needed to be replaced and the jacket he wore could certainly be outclassed in a second-hand thrift store.

Running his fingers through his hair he let his eyes scan the dinner. There were several booths that backed up to the one he was sitting on and they were mostly full. On the other side of the aisle sat a long counter with twelve seats. Several old men sat at the counter discussing the politics of the day and spouting off their own views of the world.

"Billy, turn up the TV. They're talking about the kid from Newton," chirped one of the old men who had not bothered to take off his coat.

The TV flashed a banner headline across the bottom of the screen that said BREAKING NEWS in bold red letters. A shaking camera tried to focus on the steps of the Court House where a podium had been set up. From the TV came the familiar voice of the local news anchor.

"Good Morning. We're interrupting your regularly scheduled program to provide you with an update on the trial of Calvin Wise. The jury has come back with a verdict of not guilty. Needless to say, this will come as a shock to all who have been following this case."

The screen flashed to an image of several suited men walking out of the Court House and approaching the podium.

"Now to get comment from our expert legal analyst, Dreck Slader."

"Thanks, John. I must say that I'm amazed at the verdict for this case. The legal team assembled by Wise's father listed like a who's who of trial law in Boston, but most people felt they would be lucky to get manslaughter in a plea deal. Now they've taken the case to trial and won. Just amazing."

"Approaching the podium is the district attorney. Let's listen in."

Stepping to the front of the podium was a stern and hard looking woman who appeared to be in her fifties. Falau shifted in his seat and leaned closer to hear the comments coming from the TV, while the old men gave their opinions on how such a travesty of justice could take place.

"Good afternoon. As representatives of the state of Massachusetts and the district attorney's office, I cannot stress how disappointed myself and my staff is at the outcome of this trial. As has been well documented in the papers, several times we have requested that the sitting judge re-examine his rulings during the case, but were met with answers of no. The district attorney's office will re-examine the case and see if there is any way in which we can reopen this case or find the defendant connected with any of the other murders that were linked to the application he used. We will not sleep until the people of the commonwealth see justice done."

The woman stepped away from the microphone, ready to walk away without taking any questions. But bursting past her before she could get her bearings was Calvin Wise and his team of attorneys.

"I told you all it wasn't me! I am innocent! I didn't do a thing. You will all be lucky if I don't sue you for slander. I told you! I told you!" barked the brash young man while wagging his finger at the camera.

The camera cut abruptly away from the scene at the Court House and focused back on the anchorman sitting at his desk.

"Well there were some strong words from Calvin Wise after being found not guilty. It is also clear that the district attorney is visibly upset with the outcome of this case," said the anchorman. "We heard her mention the numerous times the judge made rulings during the case to keep various pieces of information inadmissible. Some have even questioned if there could be action taken with the state bar for some of the dubious conduct of Judge Steinburg during this trial. But for now, Calvin Wise is walking free from the Boston District Court House. Please check back with us at 12, 6 and 11 for the most up-to-date information on this case and all the other news, weather and sports. We now return you to your regularly scheduled program."

The TV flashed back to a game show with a young man dressed like a chicken jumping up and down for what seemed like far too low a sum of money by Falau's standards.

"What an asshole," mumbled Falau under his breath, turning back to his cup of coffee.

"You're right, he is an asshole. I would have held out for $300 to get in the chicken suit," said the familiar voice of an old friend.

Jumping to his feet Falau stood face to face with his old friend Tyler and hugged him tightly. Tyler was quick to return the hug and patted Falau hard on the back.

The young man named Tyler was impeccably dressed wearing a suit and a stylish overcoat. His hair was slicked back and he looked like he could have stepped from the pages of a men's fashion magazine.

"How you are doing, man?" asked Tyler.

"Great now that I'm seeing you. I was beginning to think you were gone for good."

"No way, man. Just been on assignment. You know how it is." Tyler slid into the other side of the booth, unbuttoning his coat and signaling the waitress for a cup of coffee.

"So, is this a social visit or a work visit?" questioned Falau.

A slow smile crept across Tyler's face as he looked up without lifting his head.

"Work. I was thinking you might be ready for another go around. Are you?"

"I could use some work," replied Falau with a flat expression on his face. Picking up the pack of cigarettes from the table he tapped the side of the pack, dislodging one from the other side. As his fingers took hold of it he tried to read the expression on Tyler's face. Was the mission easy or hard? What were they going to ask him to do?

"You know those things will kill you," commented Tyler, looking down at his hands on the pack of cigarettes.

"You too? Seems like everyone is up my ass about smoking."

"Maybe you should quit?"

"And give up all the stimulating conversation that comes out of it? Never!"

Tyler chuckled and leaned back in the booth. Falau could feel his eyes working their way over him, assessing if he was ready to take on a mission.

"I have a serious question for you Falau," said Tyler, a hard edge to his voice. "I need to know how far you're willing to go in your work. Do you just want to bring the goods back, or do you want to take care of everything? Each has its own advantages and disadvantages, but the money is significantly different."

Falau stared hard at his old friend. The question was valid and worthy. The simple way to ask it was, "Will you kill for money?"

"That's a big question for eleven in the morning."

"We have some things that need taking care of and two came up that had your name on them. We just need to know where you stand at this time."

Taking a deep breath, his eyes drifted out the window to a Lincoln town car that sat across the street in which sat two men in suits.

"Your friends are still in your hip pocket I see."

"Don't change the subject," Tyler said in a firm but calm tone. "What do you want to do?'

Falau took the pack of cigarettes and tossed them to the side of the table next to the window and rubbed his face hard with his hand. "I can bring you what you need, but that's all. I can't go the full way for you.

It's just not in me. Is that going to be a problem? Should I be looking for a new line of work?"

"It's no problem. We would rather know where you stand and what your position is than have you get out into the field and have to come back after an incomplete mission. Give me a week and I will make contact with you again. I need to go back to the bosses and iron out what your task will be."

"What if I never want to go the full distance?" asked Falau, looking down at the table and not really wanting to know the answer to the question.

"If you're good at what you do there is no problem being a specialist with us. We would rather have people that are exceptional at what they do than okay at doing numerous things. Don't worry, we're not going to dump you from the system. You have proven yourself to us."

Falau's head slowly rose and a smile crossed his face.

"You're a good friend, Tyler. Thanks for all your help."

Tyler slid to the edge of the seat and stood up. Reaching into his pocket he pulled out a ten-dollar bill and dropped it on the table, then placed his hand on Falau's shoulder and looked down at him.

"No problem, man. Just be ready for something in the next week or so. Oh, and you can pick up the coffee next time."

Falau smiled as his friend made his way out the door of the diner, causing the familiar ring of the bell positioned above it. Taking a sip from his coffee the big man again wondered what he was getting himself into. Not knowing what was coming was always the hardest part.

Chapter 3

The lights were dim even for the gritty standard of a dive bar. The whole room seemed to be a throwback to the 1970's, trapped in a time warp where interior design had shuddered to a grinding halt. The bar was long and thin not much deeper than thirty-feet. The bar ran down one side of the room about halfway, and at the back of the room sat a few tables next to an old juke-box. All the seats were covered with imitation red leather that took on a burgundy color in the low light. The wood was all dark and as cheap as the linoleum that lay shriveled on top of the bar. A few patrons sat scattered at the bar drinking their daily fill.

"What the hell are we doing in here?" questioned the elderly black man, the years of hard living etched into his face. His eyes had lost their light and the creases in his face were long and deep. They had stories to tell, and he was normally all too willing to share them if the listener picked up the tab.

"What? How can you have a problem with this place?" Falau popped back, taking the glass of whiskey away from his lips.

"Five dollars for a whiskey and soda! You must be kidding me. We could get a whole bottle for the cost of just a few drinks here."

Rolling his eyes Falau took a sip from his drink and placed it back on the bar. "Don't worry about it. I'm covering the bill. Just drink up."

"It ain't about who's paying. I just feel strange in a place like this. It's all rich lookin'. What's wrong with the stoop, anyway?"

"Grady, it's cold out. I have the money. Let's just live it up for a while."

Grady gulped down the contents of his glass and banged it down on the bar, causing the few heads in the room to turn toward him. Falau lifted his hand to let the bartender know everything was fine and there would be no problem in his bar.

Grady lowered his voice and leaned into his friend, a strong smell of alcohol on his breath. "That's another thing I don't like. You were days away from getting kicked out of your apartment. Then you disappear for a few days. Now you have money. What the hell is that all about?"

"Well—"

Grady's hand shot up, placing a stop sign in front of Falau. "Don't tell me. I know it can't be good and the last thing I need is to be an accessory after the fact."

Letting out a soft chuckle Falau motioned to the bartender for two more glasses of whiskey.

"You think this is funny? Well I know you're doing something that's wrong and you mark my words you will get your ass burned by it eventually. Nobody comes up with a pocket full of cash like you did unless they're doing something illegal!"

The bartender placed the drinks in front of the two men with a smile. "You guys okay? I don't need any problems in my bar."

"No problems," interjected Grady before Falau could speak. "Just trying to talk some sense into this guy, but it won't get out of hand."

"That's all I needed to hear," said the bartender before he turned away, lifting the back of his shirt to expose a handgun Falau had already picked up on.

"Grady, I appreciate you looking out for me but trust me when I say I am not doing anything that will land me up in jail. I have things under control."

Turning to Falau and casting a hard stare that seemed to look more through him than at him, Grady nodded his head up and down slowly. "I've heard a lot of guys around the hood talk like that all my life. You know what happens to all of them?"

Falau shook his head indicating no.

"They end up in the joint. I know you're a tough guy Falau, but you're way too good looking to do time. Don't be stupid. Poor is much better than in jail."

"I understand."

"You better understand."

Chapter 4

The door of the apartment opened with a clunk as it slapped against the wall behind it. Falau staggered through the door doing the walk of the drunken man, just as he had so many times before. His eyes scanned over the apartment with disgust. He preferred to drink his money rather than spend it on furniture or a better place to live.

The apartment was one of many in the brownstone buildings that sat on Massachusetts Avenue in Boston, Massachusetts. The apartment consisted of one room with a bathroom attached. A small kitchen sat at one side of the room, and at the other end was a mattress on the floor, a lamp without a shade next to it, and a tattered sofa covered by a sheet. The carpet was worn down. The old TV sat on an egg crate. A mismatched coffee table held a few old magazines, an overflowing ashtray, and a box of 9mm bullets.

Stumbling across the room his coat dropped from his shoulders to the floor. Reaching the far side of the room, standing on his mattress he pulled the window open to let in some fresh air. Wiggling himself onto the windowsill he felt safe from falling due to the fire escape that protected him.

Looking down at the street through half-closed eyes the big man fought the desire to let his mind wander. Nothing good could come from that, only a whole lot of bad.

Taking a cigarette from the pack in his pocket he cupped his hands and lit the tip, taking a long slow drag. A few gang members ran up the street as the sounds of police sirens echoed off far away buildings. Falau knew there was no way the cops would ever catch the kids with that much of a lead and a far more intimate knowledge of the back allies and buildings than the police would ever have.

Taking the cigarette from his mouth he held it in front of him. "Weakness," he whispered to himself. "If I can't stop doing this, how can I do anything?"

The familiar flow of depression and emotional self-abuse started again. Sweat began to bead on his neck. The pattern was all too clear and the big man braced himself for what was about to come.

His head started to throb and flashing images started to reverberate in his mind. The flashbacks had haunted him for years and tonight was another night he would have to grit his teeth and bear the torture of his past.

Shaking his head rapidly he banged it back hard against the window frame in an effort to stop the images and sounds from infiltrating his mind. Flicking the cigarette out the window to the ground below Falau fell back into the room onto his bed.

A sharp flash raced across his mind of a woman's face. Her eyes were soft and her hair was long. She smiled gently at him, causing him to feel warm and content. Without warning blood started to drip down from her hairline, causing long red streaks over her face. Her eyes went blank and lifeless.

Falau's body jerked hard in his bed knocking over the lamp. As the flashbacks escalated they always got longer and more intense. Despite having no control of the images and sounds in his head, Falau was aware of what was happening to him but he was helpless to stop it.

A woman leaned against the passenger side door inside a car, smiling across to him. The radio was distant and soft. Leaning forward she hugged him and whispered in his ear. It was all perfect as she leaned back into her spot against the door. The light turned green and they pulled into the intersection. Turning to look at the young beauty he knew was far above his station, he caught a glimpse of the pickup truck out the passenger side window over her shoulder. No time to yell. No time to warn her. No time to brace himself. The grill of the pickup truck impacted the car where the front and back doors met on the passenger side, causing the woman to lurch across the car, her head colliding with a crunch against the steering wheel, her hair wrapping around it before she recoiled backward.

Falau gasped for air as he thrashed in his bed. Another image flashed in front of his eyes of the bloody lifeless face saying, "You killed me. It's your fault." Her face started to melt with the rush of blood that flowed from her wounds all over her body and her eyes turned a cold hard gray. "Why? Why did you do this to me?" she whispered without any movement of her mouth.

Falau's eyes burst open as he tried to control his breathing through the tears and fear that were overcoming him. Reaching out to find the woman, all his hands found was emptiness.

"No. Come back," he spat out through his labored breathing, his heart rate not slowing and his body feeling like it had just been in the accident that surged through his mind. "I need you."

Rolling to the side the big man punched hard down on his pillow, pounding it several times to let out at least some of his frustration.

"You killed me," whispered a voice in the back of his head, letting him know that the flashbacks could come back at any time.

Grabbing the half-drunk bottle of whiskey from the floor next to his bed he downed four big mouthfuls without removing his lips from the bottle. If drinking himself unconscious would keep the demons away he was willing to try it. Again, he brought the bottle up to his mouth but this time the tears fell harder and with more emotion of sadness than fear. He sipped the whiskey in a long-fought battle over his emotions and the flashbacks. He was not willing to go back to that hell again tonight.

Finishing the remainder of the bottle in one long gulp, he fell onto his face on the bed and wept uncontrollably, whispering, "Please stop. I'm sorry. Please. Please stop. I'm so sorry."

Chapter 5

The morning sun broke through the window and shone onto Falau's eyelids, causing him to roll over and bury his head in the pillow. The spent whiskey bottle fell to the floor with a clanking sound and rolled a few feet away.

A long, steady groan came from the man who dreaded to open his eyes. The pounding in his head was a direct result of the amount of whiskey he'd drunk. His body ached and reminded him of his limitations with alcohol. Even for a seasoned drinker he pushed the bounds of consumption in a furious attempt to control his mind. Now his body was paying him back for what he had put it through.

Knock Knock Knock!

The infernal sound split through his head. *Who could be so careless to pound on my door at this time of the morning,* thought the big man. Cracking his eyes to see his alarm clock he saw the time was 11:22 am. Purging air between his lips they flapped, and he grunted as he pulled himself into a sitting position in no rush to find out who was at the door.

Knock. Knock Knock.

"I know you're in there," chimed the familiar teasing voice of Tyler.

"Hold on!" Falau called back, feeling every word cut through his head like a knife. Of all the people he knew, Tyler was the last one he wanted to see while in this condition. Shuffling to the door he grabbed a bottle of water off the coffee table and took a sip, hoping to calm the nauseous feeling that had overcome him since the time he'd stood up.

"I can smell the booze on you from out here," snapped Tyler with little sympathy in his voice.

Falau undid the lock and opened the door to a well put together Tyler standing on the threshold. "Well you have an extraordinary nose, because I haven't had a drink since last night."

"Still drinking? Don't you think it's time to get your shit together with that?"

Placing a cigarette in his mouth Falau sat down on the sofa and pulled the sheet off the back. "First cigarettes, now booze? What are you, the fun police?"

"How fun can it be if it's killing you?"

"A lot of fun. Next thing you know you're going to be telling me what to eat. You did your friend thing so you can just back off and not feel guilty when I go down the hole."

"Sorry friend, but you're not going down in the hole for another sixty years, and if I have to be on your ass for all sixty years I will be. Consider me not just a friend, but a mother!"

Choking on the cigarette due to laughing from Tyler's joke, Falau nodded his head up and down in agreement. "I know I have to knock some of this stuff off, but there's a lot going on that makes it hard."

"Jennifer?"

Instantly Falau's jaw tightened and his lips curled hard. Forcing the cigarette into his mouth he took a long draw and looked at the floor before exhaling. Anger filled his body and mind.

"How do you know about Jennifer?"

"We know everything. You know that."

"You have no right to know about her."

"We were not looking for her. She came up during the normal research when they were seeing if you would be good to work with. I can assure you that you have all of our sympathies."

Leaning back against the sofa and letting the ash drop from his cigarette without regard for where it landed, he shot Tyler a stern and hard look. But it seemed to have no effect on the calm and cool professional.

"I don't want to talk about that."

"Understood. I'm here on business anyway. I have a job for you."

The anger drifted away and a smile replaced the hardness on Falau's face. A job meant money, and also meant Tyler still believed in him despite what he looked like this morning.

"Good. Sit down and tell me about it."

"No thanks... I don't want to stick to anything," Tyler said sarcastically.

Letting out a loud laugh that echoed through his head, the hung-over Falau enjoyed the sharp teasing from his friend. He watched as Tyler's eyes ran over the apartment like it had done in the past. The look on his face was not one of amusement; it was more like frustration. Tyler had his life together and Falau did not. Falau was living like he had nothing to live for, and Tyler was living the life of a man who had everything for which to live. Yet, when they were younger it was Falau who lead the way and Tyler followed. *How could two men who started in the same place end up in such different places?* thought Falau.

"You sure you want me for the job?" Falau asked with total seriousness in his voice. "I know I'm not the guy you hoped I would be. I'm not sure why you even put up with me. You're risking a lot to give me any kind of job. Why?"

"I believe in you. I know what you're capable of. I know when the chips are down that you will do everything in your power to get a job done right. I know the last thing you want is to let me down. Basically, you're a good guy with an amazing skill set."

Tyler turned and walked across the room and looked out the window at the people below and shook his head. "You're not like them. It's Tuesday morning at 11:00am and nobody is at work. Yet I saw five places on Massachusetts Ave looking for help." Pointing out the window Tyler raised his voice. "They have been beaten down. They have given up, thinking they don't have a chance to get out. But that's not you. You're just stuck in the past."

Turning back to Falau Tyler adjusted his jacket and placed his hands out in front of him. "You choose this."

Something deep in Falau stirred, but not anger or aggression. It was far worse than that. It was something that hits when someone else is exactly right about what is wrong with you. The kind of thing there is no argument for. Falau struggled to think of something to say but knew it was all just bullshit. Tyler had him pegged and there was nothing false in what he said. Instead, the big man looked to the ground and slowly nodded in agreement.

"If you don't find a way to let go of the past then you're going to end up in prison or dead. You know that's true. There is no other outcome. I'm giving you the chance to be one of the good guys. The judges and the system want you to be the man to bring people back for justice. We all know what you can do. We have seen what you can do. But your mind has to be sharp. You get picked up for a mistake, and you're on your own. You know we are not some court house. We retry the scumbags who initially get let off, and then we dish out justice. You're part of that justice. You need to start feeling good about that and all the people it helps and the many lives it saves."

"I get it, but it's easier said than done. Just know I'm working on it." Falau flicked the cigarette to the floor without putting it out.

Pointing to the lit cigarette that sat nestled in the carpet, Tyler shook his head. "That's the stuff I'm talking about. The old Falau I knew would never do something like that. You're taking a chance on burning the whole place down by being stupid. Come on man, you're better than that!"

"Okay! I understand! Can you just get on to business, or is that off the table now?"

"No, it's not off the table," replied Tyler, turning away and walking to the door. "But if you fuck this up then there will be nothing more. The judges can't look the other way about your life unless the missions get fulfilled."

"That's fair," Falau said, sliding himself up to the edge of the couch and leaning forward, looking for details about what the mission was.

"This one is kind of standard. Not too much risk. No travel. Best part is it pays $25,000. We need the target brought back alive and everything has to be kept quiet."

"$25,000? That's good. I can do quiet. I have never been an explosions and gunfire guy anyway."

Picking up the box of 9mm ammunition Tyler smiled and shook it. "I can tell you're not a gunfire guy. If you ever want to move up from a toy gun let me know. I can get you something."

"Hey, the 9mm is just fine. Besides, I got it from an old partner. It has sentimental value as well as killing value," replied Falau while battling to keep a straight face with his off-color joke. Pulling the Ruger SR9C from its holster, the brushed metal top of the gun shone in the light. The bottom was black and had an extended handle for a firm grip. The weapon was small by anyone's standard, but Falau loved it.

"Okay, you keep bouncing off windshields and taking five shots to get the job done, and I will stick with the .45."

"Some guys just need to have a big one," said Falau with a smirk, remembering his old partner. "So, what are the details and when can I start?"

Tyler again made his way to the window and looked down at the street below. The car with the two men in suits that followed him everywhere was parked directly across the street. "My FBI friends are with me, like usual, so we can't talk here. I'm sure by now they have their sound system set up to listen in on us. Hi guys!" barked Tyler, looking down on the men and chuckling as they quickly pulled away from the curb.

"Okay, if you're really ready for this one we need to take a little ride. Like always there are eyes on us everywhere, and that's just the way we want it. I'm sure you've been followed a lot lately because of dealing with me. So, let's get out of here and we can talk in the car."

Falau stood up and made a b-line for the door, and grabbing his coat said, "Let's go!"

Chapter 6

Climbing into the new black sedan Falau felt as if every time he saw Tyler he was driving a different car. Today it was a BMW that spared no expense. With all that it had going for it in the looks department, Falau was sure that under the hood there would be nothing left to desire. Tyler needed a car that could perform in all situations, and not only that, but be able to do it at the drop of a hat.

The big man reached across and put on his seatbelt as Tyler started the car. Tyler's brand of driving was unique to say the least. He could draw out someone following him with the numerous starts, stops and turns he would take, and bouncing around the car was nothing new when you sat in the passenger seat with Tyler at the wheel.

The sharply dressed man placed the key into the ignition and turned it, bringing the car to life. He pressed the gas two times causing a simple but pronounced roar from under the hood. Sliding on his sunglasses he dropped the car into gear and launched away from the curb in a flash.

Cruising up Massachusetts Avenue he took a hard right without giving a signal and then a sharp left into an alley. Falau looked over, sure that his friend had gone mad trying to fit his car down the tight unmarked street. If they were to get stuck Falau doubted that even if he climbed out the window he could get out of the car.

Reaching the end of the alley he spotted a large garage door built into the side of a building. Tyler reached into his console and took out what looked like a remote garage door opener. He hit the button with a smile and the door started to roll up.

"Membership has its privileges," he quipped, quoting an old TV ad.

He pressed down on the gas again and the car rolled into what looked like a one-car garage, the door automatically closing behind them.

"What, no crazy driving this time? I was just getting used to that." Falau reached for the door handle but was quickly stopped by Tyler.

"We are not there yet. Just sit tight," he instructed. The bottom of the car started to shake and suddenly there was the feeling of movement, like an elevator going down. The ride was far from smooth, and a loud crack sounded as it came to a stop. Behind the BMW a door opened again to a room approximately double the size of the elevator. Tyler put the car in reverse and backed up into the room. The two men watched the elevator door close and heard it making its way back up.

"Alright. What the hell is this?" questioned Falau while staring at Tyler, confused and impressed at the same time.

"Boston is a rich city for some. This is a private parking garage for people who don't want their cars seen by anyone. You don't even know the other people in the garage. You have your own private spot and nobody has access to it but you, not even the management. Who knows what kind of stuff is hidden in this garage."

"Probably bodies. Lots and lots of bodies," said Falau with a smirk, trying to make light of the situation. "So what are we doing here?"

"You're getting a new car."

Tyler opened the door and exited the car into a dimly lit room, Falau close behind. Reaching into his pocket Tyler pulled out his cell phone and entered what looked like a phone number, but when he hit send the wall at the far end of the room started to rise.

Anticipation filled Falau's mind at what Tyler had in store for him. It had been years since he'd had a car and now he was going to get one with all the latest gadgets Tyler had been working on.'

As the door crept higher, the smile on Falau's face was once again replaced by confusion. When the wall was finally gone, a red 2000 Dodge Caravan with peeling paint sat in front of him.

"Ta Da!" mocked Tyler, waving his hands out to the side. "Complete with cassette player and hand-crank windows."

"You must be kidding?"

"If you want to blend in around Boston this is the car to do it in."

"Well... I guess you're right about that."

"Besides, it's what's under the hood that matters. This isn't just your normal V6 to take the family around in. Give me more credit than that."

Falau shot a sideways glance at Tyler, wondering what surprises awaited. "Okay, I'm listening. What does she have?"

Tyler stepped away from Falau and hit a light switch that cast more light onto the car from above and below. The room was more than a showroom; it was a functional garage capable of holding a team of people to work on the car all at one time. It was impressive, and exactly what he expected from Tyler. The light also revealed the car looked worse than it had originally seemed. The paint flaked in parts, and the sealer looked as if it had eroded away from the body of the car. Falau could not help but think that if someone put this car up for sale they would be lucky to get much more than $500 for it.

"It looks like crap."

"You pop that hood and it looks normal, but deep inside it has some extras that will let you run this toddler carrier over 140mph. Let me show you the inside."

Tyler moved quickly to the driver's side door and opened it, much like a salesman pushing his target into the car. Around the front of the car he moved with purpose, climbing into the passenger side filled with excitement and grinning from ear to ear.

Falau was far less enthused by what he saw. The dashboard was covered with dust. The plastic covering the speedometer and RPM display was fogged over and made it barely visible. The radio had a cassette, just like Tyler explained, but a tape seemed to be caught inside with three inches of tape hanging out the corner. There were fast food cups and bags on the floor and a layer of crud on the console between the two front seats.

"To think that I thought the outside was bad," quipped Falau while rolling his eyes. "This time I'm afraid that *I* will stick to something."

"Relax, you big baby, it's part of the disguise. How could a guy with your history be so squeamish? Oh, and I got the joke about sticking."

Falau smiled, happy he'd returned the jab of uncleanliness to Tyler after their go around in his apartment. "Sitting in the car could cause it. I don't even have kids, and this is making me positive I don't want any."

"Well this car can do some things that the other soccer mom's cars cannot. You will be the envy of the cul-de-sac with this little number." Pointing to one of the preset buttons for the radio, Tyler continued. "See this button? Well if you hit it rapidly three times in a row the hatchback will open while you're driving. Follow that with one of the other presets, and you could drop chains, spikes, or fire out the back of the van. That could create a bit of a problem for anyone following you."

Falau smiled, knowing this was just the tip of the iceberg with Tyler. He never led off with the best stuff. He loved to build up to it.

"Great windows in this car as well. Clear and bullet-proof! Look in the rearview mirror when the back door is down and you will get a display saying how far back the next car is, as well as running its license plate. That could come in handy."

"I like that. Good for learning who's who," interrupted Falau, feeling like he had to shower some praise on his old friend after teasing him earlier.

"If you like that check this out. A cigarette lighter!"

"Yup, that's what it is," remarked Falau, trying not to sound unimpressed but waiting for Tyler to spring the surprise on him.

"Yup, it will light your smoke. Even though I don't like you smoking. But if you push it in and out three times it will do this."

The hand of the genius moved the lighter in and out three times and the side doors of the van opened. The first-row seats rolled into themselves and slid back under the second row. While the seats found their place under the last row, two machine gun turrets sprang up from where the seats once sat, one machine gun facing each way.

"Wow!" Falau exclaimed, looking back over his shoulder into the back seat. "That's amazing."

"Here's the best part. You can control where it shoots by using what is marked as the windshield wipers. I designed the wipers to automatically sense rain, so there's no need to have anything to work them. If you're trying to keep your eyes on the road just flip the wiper lever down all the way and it will lock on the closest thing to the side of the van and track it. There is no way they can hide from you. If they drop behind you the turrets will open the back door and keep shooting. No wasted bullets, because if it does not have a clean shot it will hold fire. Basically, it will kill anything you ask it to."

"Tyler, like always, you're amazing. I don't know how you do it, but you always do it. How long did all this take you?"

"I've been working on it on and off for the last year, just waiting for the right time to put it into action. But it's not complete. The air conditioning is still a bit iffy. Sometimes it works and sometimes it doesn't."

Falau laughed, slapping Tyler's shoulder, his head spinning from how something so ugly could be so amazing. "Tyler, I can honestly say I feel as if there is very little that could ever harm me if I'm in this van. It is my fortress."

Tyler smiled and leaned back in the seat. "Only one more thing to do."

"What's that?"

Tyler reached into his coat pocket and took out a set of keys and flipped them to Falau.

"Drive!"

Chapter 7

‒‒‒‒‒‒‒

The van pulled out onto the street with a squeal of the tires. The slightest depression of the gas pedal lurched the car forward past the car to the left.

"She's just begging to be driven fast," Falau stated, taking his foot off the gas. "It would be nice to see what she can really do. Maybe we can open her up."

"That does sound like fun, but getting a ticket at this point in the mission and having the car impounded could screw everything up," Tyler said with a coy smile. "No matter how much we would both love to test this van out, now is not the time. Let's take her up on the highway and you can get a better feel, but within reason."

At the first sight of an on-ramp Falau gave the gas a quick push, steering the car to the inside and drawing a look from the corner of Tyler's eye. On the highway, the van moved smooth and crisp, and the handling of the big minivan felt more like a sports car. It responded well to the gas and brakes. If not for its overall ugly look, it would be the perfect sports car.

"Get off here," commanded Tyler, pointing to the off-ramp a hundred yards ahead.

Reaching the end of the ramp the light turned yellow and Falau started to press the brake pedal.

"Hit it! You can make it. Go! Go! Go!" barked Tyler, giving the big man the chance he'd been waiting for to test what the minivan could do.

Upon hearing the command Falau's eyes fluttered and he gripped the steering wheel hard. "No, not now!" he whispered to himself as he felt the flashback coming on. Sweat started to bead on his forehead and the road ahead became blurry. Shaking his head to fight away the demons he attempted to look composed, but it was no use.

"It was your fault," she whispered from the recesses of his mind. "You killed me, and now you're going to kill your friend."

"No!" barked Falau, shaking the steering wheel in anger. The woman's face invaded his vision and looked into his eyes with her own lifeless eyes, the blood flowing from her hair-line.

"Falau!" yelled Tyler, placing one hand on the dashboard and the other grabbing the coat of his friend. "Brake! Brake!"

The hard yanking of Tyler's hand on the collar of his coat pulled Falau back into reality and away from the tortures of his mind.

Cars raced side to side in front of them at the intersection. His feet pushed down hard on the brake causing the car to skid to a stop just inches from going out into oncoming the traffic. The van came to rest at an angle after the skid, and all eyes were on the men who'd disrupted this calm suburban off-ramp.

"What the hell was that all about?"

Falau's hands were still gripping the steering wheel tight. He had to concentrate to remove his fingers one by one. The skid had caused Tyler to slide in his seat so now he was leaning against the passenger side door.

"Sorry... I wasn't paying attention. You caught me off guard," lied Falau without making eye contact with his friend.

"Bull shit! Can you handle this mission? I am not interested in sending you into something that gets you killed."

"I'm fine... it was just a skid. Relax," Falau said, trying to sound confident but instead stammering like a nervous schoolboy asking for his first date.

"You've got me worried about you," said Tyler. The light turned green and he looked at Falau. "Take a left here and turn onto Rosewood about a mile up on the right."

The two sat in silence, processing what had just happened and trying to make sense of it all. Falau wondered if the little flashback had ended his mission before it had ever started.

Turning onto Rosewood the car slowly rolled down the street before reaching a mechanic's garage at the far end.

"Pull in there," ordered Tyler, rolling down his window as Falau pulled into the first open parking spot he found. "You want to tell me what that was all about?"

"I told you it was nothing."

"Falau, I have known you too long for you to just say nothing after that. It was something, and you better start trusting me. I might just be the only person that has your best interests at heart. I don't even think you do."

"Why don't you just back the hell off?" snapped Falau, turning a hard face to Tyler. "You yap at me like you're in charge of me but you never talk about what you're all about. I know you from years ago, but I know nothing of you now. You're just the guy who pops up with a job. It's not like we do anything other than that, definitely nothing friends would do. Normal friends would play poker or go to a Red Sox game, but unless it's work you're a ghost in my life."

The car fell silent, the kind of silence that only happens after a bitter truth has been uttered. The entire feeling of the car changed. Even the air felt different. Comments that follow those types of moments define friendships and relationships of all kinds.

"I'm sorry. You're right," said Tyler humbly, looking over to his friend. "You're a grown man and I need to respect that. I also have to make some time to do some things out of work hours. I have a problem with that in general. I basically just see people connected to the job. You're my only friend, and I have just about managed to make that work. When this one is all finished we'll start over by taking in a Red Sox—"

Suddenly an envelope dropped onto Tyler's lap from his open window. Looking into the rearview mirror Falau saw a short man with an overcoat and a ski hat walking away from the car and up the road.

"Drive," Tyler said, a look of urgency in his eyes.

"Where to?"

"Anywhere. Just as long as we're moving."

The van pulled back into the traffic and cruised along various side streets and in and out of parking lots. Despite not being instructed to do so Falau was sure that Tyler wanted to make sure nobody was following them.

After ten minutes of tactical driving Tyler ripped into the envelope and slipped out the contents. Unfolding the single piece of paper he started to laugh.

"What's so funny?" asked Falau, knowing Tyler was not one for levity when it came to information about missions.

"The paper has only three words on it."

"So, what does it say?"

"Calvin Wise alive."

"Calvin Wise? Isn't that the kid who just got off after killing that girl?"

"That's exactly who it is. Your option of mission was between him and one other person the judges were looking at. Looks like Calvin just won the worst contest of his life."

The van moved in and out of the traffic with ease as Falau kept one eye on the road and one on Tyler. The uncomfortable feeling that Tyler was withholding information started to permeate into Falau's mind. He could always tell when Tyler was holding back.

"Okay, what's the catch? This guy is in my backyard and just some college kid. Anyone could pick him up. Why me?"

Tyler nervously shifted in his seat and tapped his ring on the center console. "It's not really a catch. It's more like a risk. This kid Wise is the son of John Wise, a very rich man who comes from old money. He took that old money and turned it into billions with the dot com explosion in the late 1990's. Turn right here."

Falau cut the wheel before passing the street. The tires dug into the road and screeched as they made a turn that no other minivan could have made.

"Nothing like waiting until the last second!"

Tyler laughed. "You wanted to see what the van could do? Well, I figured I could show you in bits and pieces. That was turning. Anyway, John Wise knows everyone in Massachusetts. He contributes to all the campaigns. He's a townie. This guy could do or say anything he wanted and nobody would say a thing. He is the power in the state that nobody sees. If he wants he can control just about anything. Little Calvin Wise knows how much power daddy has, so he knows he can do anything including, killing people. That trial was dirty before anyone even hit the court room."

Falau nodded in fake agreement, not fully understanding what Tyler was talking about.

"Why is it I have never heard of this guy until the kid went on trial? The father was never involved in anything that I can remember."

"He was involved with every major thing that has gone on in this city for the last thirty years," Tyler said as a matter of fact. "Every city has these guys. It's only just a few in each place. They are never public. They are way too smart for that. They stay underground and manipulate everything from afar. Most of the time these guys are not even in it for money. It's all about the power."

Falau smiled, not taking his eyes off the road. "Comes in handy if your kid is a psycho killer."

"You got that right. The worst part for you is that he has an inside link with every police department and court all over the state. Basically, they act like his security. The cops on the street are not on the take, but they are told he is at high risk of being attacked by terrorists because of some history they say he has with a counter-terrorism group. It's all bull shit, but it does the job. The guy is above the law and as we both saw the kid is above the law too."

"So, there are always eyes on the kid?"

"Now you're getting it. To take this kid, it will be more than just grabbing him out of some dorm room. He now lives at home and the house has guards and attack-dogs. The police drive by the house constantly and there are still news cameras popping up. It's basically hell for what you are trying to do."

Falau slapped the shoulder of his long-time friend. "Sounds like my kind of mission, Tyler. It *is* my kind of mission."

Chapter 8

Tyler continued to give instructions of various twists and turns until they had been in the car for over an hour. It was clear he was again making sure they had not been followed. No matter how much he said the federal officers who followed him were fools, Tyler was always sure to put caution first. Falau admired his attention to detail and his focus on what was at hand. No simple mistake would lead to Tyler's undoing.

Following the instructions Falau found himself at a gate leading up to a house high on a hill. A security pad was located just outside the gate.

Tyler hopped out of the passenger seat. "Sorry man, no offense but I can't let you know the code."

"No offense taken. Besides, if I wanted to get in I would just climb the fence."

Tyler laughed and hunched over the key-pad, screening his hands as he entered in the code. The large wrought iron gadget slowly started to slide open. Falau watched as the gate did not wiggle at all as it opened, meaning it had to be seriously reinforced. Tyler would not have gone to all the trouble to have the gate and wall built if a bump from a car could take out the gate with little effort.

Falau started to pull up the driveway, and noticed small cuts in the asphalt. Not needing to ask what they were for, he knew that the driveway had been equipped with some kind of security system, most likely concrete pylons that would pop up when triggered to do so. It was a simple yet efficient way to stop someone from following you in or out of the house. There was no telling how many of these surprises Tyler had rigged up, both within the grounds and inside the house.

"Beautiful home. I assume it's yours," commented Falau.

"Yes, it is. I got a great deal. You could say I know some people that helped me out."

"I bet. Looks like you have some nice security items here in the driveway. Have you had problems with taking the job home with you."

"No, thank God. It's been smooth sailing as far as that is concerned. But I don't like taking any chances. Besides, bringing riff-raff like you around here, who knows who will come charging after me?"

A great belly laugh rolled from Falau, catching him off guard. It had been a long time since he had genuinely felt this good. Being back a part of something was giving him purpose and providing him something to look forward to.

At the top of the driveway a three-car garage sat below the house. The door to the far left slowly started to open.

"Did you do that?" questioned Falau.

"Yup. Don't worry. Just pull in."

The van slipped into the parking spot and the door softly closed behind them to reveal a screen attached to the back of it that was linked to a camera focused on the driveway. As Tyler and Falau got out of the van they looked at the screen, seeing that nobody had followed them.

"Right up here," said Tyler walking up two steps and unlocking a door that led to a hallway.

The two men worked their way into a kitchen that looked as if it was made for a master chef rather than a guy in Tyler's kind of work. Pots and pans hung from a suspended rack above the island. There were large cutting and preparation areas. A propane grill was even built into one of the counters.

"Wow. This is one hell of a house. The kitchen is bigger than my whole apartment."

"It's nice. I wish I could cook better. Honestly, I don't really cook here at all. I do more work-related things in here. Come on, there's no time to waste. Follow me."

Pulling a key from his pocket he started unlocking a plain white door that anyone would think was a simple broom closet, and as the door swung open it appeared to be just that. Tyler reached out and grabbed his friend by the arm, pulled him into the closet and closed the door.

In the darkness Falau heard Tyler speak.

"Yes, my dear, 2, 4, 6, 3, 1."

Suddenly the room began to move and shake its way down, touching the bottom in less than ten seconds. The door to the bizarre elevator was opened again by Tyler.

The room was dark and Tyler charged headlong into it. Falau struggled to let his eyes adjust to the darkness, but with little success.

"One second. Where is it? Just a minute. Okay, got it!" exclaimed Tyler as he flipped the switch to the lights of the room.

"Oh my God!" muttered Falau, trying to understand all he was seeing.

The lights had exposed a giant lab that was at least two times the footprint of the home itself. There were areas for all types of experiments and developments of whatever Tyler wanted. At the far end of the room sat a car that was being modified. To the left was an area that appeared to be a chemistry work-station. A ballistics range just to his side. All of it seemed to be a total mess and out of control, but he was sure that, like any great scientist, Tyler knew exactly where everything was and exactly what it was for.

"Not bad, huh?" exclaimed Tyler.

"How big a team do you have working down here with you?" asked the big man

"Just me."

"Just you? No other people are helping you? How are you keeping track of all of this stuff?"

"You know me... I find a way. But don't worry about all that now. I brought you down here to show you some goodies I have for you to work with."

"Now you're talking."

Tyler led the way, waving a hand for his friend to follow. "We need to start you off with some new clothing. Take a look at what I have for you here."

Sliding open a drawer, a stack of shirts and pants were exposed that looked exactly like ones Falau had at home, albeit they were crumpled up in a ball on his floor.

"They look just like yours, but these are better. These are made with a thread that acts as a recording device for audio and video. The buttons are the cameras. If you're looking to get a confession out of that little brat, he may spill the beans and then you have it on tape to show to the judges. It will record everything you say and do from the moment you put it on and upload to our secret servers."

"I'll make sure not to trash you while I'm wearing it."

"Oh, and it is not something we can use to monitor you, so if you're in trouble we can't see it until after something happens."

"Got it."

Sliding the next drawer open Tyler removed a cell phone and held it up.

"You're going to like this one. Check it out." Holding up the cell phone he pointed it to the far wall. "Just hold the volume up button and the power button together." Suddenly an arch of electricity shot out of the phone, breaking some of the stone wall across the room. "You will get two shocks like that per charge. Like any cell phone, if the battery is low it will not work right. Oh, and it will work like a regular phone. Keep the long distance to a minimum."

"This thing is awesome. Almost worth getting into a problem just to see how it works."

Tyler's eyebrow rose without him lifting his head.

"Almost worth it, Tyler!"

"Good. No need for unwanted confrontation. Hey, check out these sunglasses."

Tyler tossed the glasses to Falau who plucked them out of midair. Flipping them open he put them on his face, adjusting them slightly.

"They seem very normal, don't they?" questioned Tyler as he walked across the room. "But normal glasses can't do this."

Flipping the lights off, Falau saw the world in night vision. All objects appeared to be outlined in green and he could see every slight movement that Tyler made. Falau marveled, realizing that he was able to see better and more detail in the room with the help of the night vision sunglasses than with his own eyes in normal daylight.

"Tyler, you have outdone yourself with this. I can make out every little thing."

"They are very effective. You can also use them to drive and get the same results. So just turn off the lights on the car on a back road with no streetlights and only you will be able to see everything."

Tyler flipped the lights back on and Falau removed the glasses.

"Just one more thing. The other day I saw that little 9mm you like to carry. I was giving you a hard time about it, just having some fun. But I want you to have the power you need if things get too hot. So, I made some adjustments for you."

"What? How could you make adjustments for me?" asked Falau.

"Oh, I went back and broke into your apartment to get the gun and replace it with another. I have the real one right here. Sorry for breaking in."

"Tyler, that gun had sentimental value for me from my first mission."

"I know. But it's still the same gun with just a few improvements that will keep you from being dead. No matter how much sentimental value it has, it will not help you if you're dead."

"Fair enough."

Tyler removed the weapon from a desk to their side. He raised the gun and shot it across the length of the room, impacting the target and blowing it to pieces.

"Stopping power! I just made the 9mm able to handle my ammo without breaking apart. My ammo packs more of a punch, and when they hit their target they explode, causing far more damage than your standard bullet. Give it a try. Shoot the car."

Tyler handed Falau the gun and stepped behind him, nodding his head as Falau checked, without speaking, to make sure it was really okay to shoot the car.

Firing two quick shots, the front driver's side quarter panel of the car erupted into flames and fell from the vehicle. The small explosion was more than Tyler had made it out to be.

"That is some real power," remarked Falau as he looked at the gun.

"Not to brag or anything, but if you get in a shootout you just need to be near the person to take them down. If you hit them, the bullet explodes on impact, meaning that as it enters the body the explosion will be happening. Stopping power."

"Ya! Stopping power!"

Chapter 9

S itting at the desk in his bedroom, Calvin Wise leaned back in his chair and took a sip from his soda. He looked around the room, enjoying all the things he had accumulated over the years.

The bedroom was ostentatious by most standards. On the wall hung a 60-inch LCD flat-screen television. Embedded in the ceiling and walls were the world's best surround sound speakers, ensuring an amazing viewing or gaming experience no matter where you sat in the room. Gaming consoles sat atop the dresser from all the major brands, such as Sony, Microsoft, and Nintendo. A king-sized bed sat in the center of the room, with the open space all around it giving a clear indication that all things in the room revolved around that one spot. An unused treadmill sat off to the side by one of the large bay windows that looked out into the backyard. There was a personal bathroom complete with hot tub and a walk-in closet that could pass for a child's bedroom in another home. The walls were covered in neon beer signs and posters of scantily clad women leaning on sports cars and motorcycles. The room as a whole looked like it belonged to an average 14-year-old boy, and not the room of an adult.

Putting the chair back to the ground, from its leaning back position, his hands reached for his laptop and opened it. Sliding the cursor over the links on his home page he stopped and hovered above the one for Hooked. Temptation filled his body and mind to click the icon and find another young woman who might want to meet for a drink.

"They're watching you and waiting for you to go on Hooked again. They will be on you before you can think and then you will live your life in prison," said a voice from the back of his mind.

"My dad will get me off," Calvin replied to the voice in his head.

"Don't do it. He can't get you off again. You have to find a new way to feel your special love."

"But I like Hooked. It works so well," Calvin said, sounding like an upset child.

"Don't whine! If you want to fix the soulless women then you need to work harder. If you want to feel them under your hands, desperate for breath, then it will take more effort from you. The question is, how much do you want their true love?"

"I want it very much. You're right, I need to be careful or there will be no more love."

The cursor slid down the page and opened to his search engine. With a few simple keystrokes, he found another suitable dating site.

Knock. Knock. Knock.

The door shook slightly as a voice asked for permission to enter the room.

Closing the laptop instantly he stared at the door, assessing if the noise had come from inside or outside his mind.

Knock. Knock. Knock.

The sound came again, but this time with more authority, and the handle of the door started to turn and the door opened approximately five inches.

The face of an older man peered through the door, though not so bold as to come fully into the room. The face was clean-shaven and handsome. He had a tan and a perfectly manicured smile that was far from natural.

"Hey, Calvin. I was going down to the kitchen and wondered if you wanted anything."

"No. If I wanted something I would get it myself or have one of the servants get it."

"I told you before, they are not servants. They work here at the house but we do not call them servants. Besides, we can go get some food without having them do it for us."

"They are lower than us. We pay them. They will do what they are told or will work somewhere else," snapped the young man, turning to the door in his chair.

The door then opened completely with a push of the older man's hand. He was in shape and toned with muscle, despite his age. His clothing was casual, but clearly expensive.

"Let's get one thing clear. I pay them for their work and I will say what they are called and whether they keep or lose their jobs. Not you. This is still my home, and from what I can see you have not contributed one dime to it, leaving you without a say in anything."

"He's against us. He doesn't understand," whispered the voice from the back of Calvin's head.

"I don't need anything to eat!"

Looking down at the desk John Wise stopped before saying what he was about to say. "Why do you have a laptop? Didn't the lawyers make it completely clear to you that using a laptop is nothing but trouble for you? Why are you taking this kind of risk this close to winning a trial?"

"A friend got it for me, okay!" screamed Calvin standing up from his chair. "Why do you have to know everything about my life? Can't you just trust me? I am a grown man, for god's sake."

"A grown man who was just on trial for killing a woman. Without me and my lawyers convincing them it was an accident you would be in prison right now!" raged the older man. "You better not be going back on one of those sites they tracked back to you. If you do, you know they will come looking for you."

Taking a couple of steps closer to his father Calvin lifted his two hands to the side of his head. "I said I didn't want anything to eat! Now leave me alone!"

Calming his tone and the volume of his voice Calvin's father put his hand on the doorknob of the room. "I got you off once, saved you from a lifetime in prison. I am not going to do it again. If you kill anyone you're going to have to face the music yourself." Closing the door softly behind him, he left Calvin standing motionless in the room.

"He wishes you were dead. He wishes he had another son," whispered the voice deep inside the young man's head. "He doesn't understand what we are doing. He doesn't understand how we are helping, spreading love and releasing the women from the sins of their mind and body. He's a problem."

Picking up his glass from the table he threw it hard against the door and yelled, "Shut up! I know!"

Grabbing the laptop off the desk he ripped the charger from the wall and stormed over to his bed. Flopping down, he opened up the screen to see that it still held his place.

"Why do you bother? The girls are never interested in you. They like me. I tell you what to say and how to say it. I am like Cyrano de Bergerac. You are just the lump of clay I talk through. You're nothing," mocked the voice that sounded angrier with each passing word.

"I will find one and I will give her my love, and you will see who the real ladies' man is," Calvin insisted, flipping through the various faces on the website.

"To do that you will need some courage, and we both know you have none of that. I have all of that."

"I can do it. Just watch and see. Then you will have to eat your words just like all the rest. No more *give Calvin the easy job. Make sure Calvin is safe. That's too much for Calvin to do.* I can do stuff, and everyone is going to see that."

Placing all his attention onto the screen of the laptop he became fully invested in what was on the display. Looking at the different faces he started to mutter to himself as if he were having conversations with the different profiles he came across.

"Whore!" he shouted, followed by, "Slut!"

"These women have no souls. They have no idea what love is. They have no idea what it is to fully give everything to your love, even down to your last heartbeat. That's love, when you let the other person squeeze the last breath from you. They need to know."

"Find one," the voice whispered from far away.

Clicking from one picture to the next he finally locked his eyes on the screen and fell motionless. Raising his hand, he brushed the picture on the screen with his fingertips and then moved them up to his lips.

"I wonder if you remember me?" he said with his voice trembling. "It's been a long time."

The picture on the screen showed a young blonde woman with dark eyes. Her face was lightly made up and she wore a gentle, soothing smile across her face. To the side of the picture the demographic information stated she lived in Boston and grew up in the area. Her hobbies were working out and helping others. She stated that she wanted to start as friends with someone and then see what happened. Her name was Victoria and she was online.

"Oh, Victoria, do you remember me from high school? I remember you. You were smart and a cheerleader. Never had time to look at a guy like me. You just sat a few seats away, chatting with the popular kids but never turning your head to even look down your nose at me! I was nothing to you, but look at you on this site with all the other sluts and whores! You need to know what love is! You need to know how much I used to think about you, wishing you would just talk to me! You need to give me all of your love and be set free!"

Punching hard down on the bed, hot tears built up in his eyes and made it hard to see the keyboard.

"Little soldiers don't cry. Little soldiers don't cry. Little soldiers don't cry..."

The cursor moved over the button that flashed with the words, "flirt now". His hand reached up and wiped the tears still in his eyes as he continually repeated his mantra to stop them falling. His finger rested on the enter button and pushed it down, popping up a dialog box with a flashing cursor inside it.

"Hi," he typed, waiting to see if there would be any response. He stared at the screen counting each second pass by.

Then it came.

"Hi. I like your profile pic."

Chapter 10

With the collar of his overcoat pulled up to block the wind from chilling his neck Falau hustled across the Quad of Tridon College in downtown Boston. Fall had started to give way to winter and the trees had dropped their leaves. The city's small animals were preparing for their annual hibernation, as would the students in a few short weeks for their winter break.

The big man was doing his best to look the part of the college professor. Wearing a button-up shirt and a sports jacket with jeans and boat shoes gave him the perfect cover for the out-of-touch and out-of-style perennially challenged college lifer. He even sported wire-rimmed glasses, a la John Lennon. His hair was slicked back, his face unshaven for one day. A simple black backpack was slung over his shoulder. Crossing in front of a window he caught sight of himself and smiled, thinking that if it were not for so many things, maybe he could have turned out this way. But he doubted it.

Cutting across the grass towards the library he hopped over a small sign that read, *Keep off the Grass*. A few students shot dirty looks his way, and one chirped up, "Read the sign."

Stopping in his tracks he turned and looked at the sign then back to the students. "Why don't you go form some kind of protest against us grass walkers before someone forces you into the real world."

The students froze, staring at who they assumed to be a professor, but his disposition was all wrong. He was aggressive and confrontational, and clearly had no interest in appeasing them or apologizing for what they felt was wrong.

"If you don't have anything to say you shouldn't just stand there. You might catch a cold," shot Falau, pressing on the students as he saw them visibly struggle to comprehend what he was saying.

"Come on," said one of the kids, and the others followed, muttering expletives about the man they'd just met and his sin against the college.

Watching them walk away Falau realized he could have just blown his cover. He knew the confrontation was a mistake and that he had to gain control of his emotions. The cover of being a college professor had to go beyond just his appearance, and he had to be able to pull it off in one-on-one conversations. If he were to be successful at this, he knew he had to play the part in every way.

"No need to let Tyler know about that one," he muttered to himself while climbing the steps of the library.

Entering the building he was met with a beehive of activity. It was far from the old-town libraries he was used to. The building was modern with natural light coming in from all sides. Just inside the front door the ceiling rose four floors, creating balconies on each floor retained by glass rails. Stairways and elevators rose from the central lobby area. To Falau the room felt more like a business office than a library, but he knew that this level of education and school was always out of his reach, both socially and financially.

Flashing his faculty ID at the student sitting at the desk reading a textbook, he walked by without pausing, just as Tyler had instructed him to do. The plan was simply to act like he owned the place so nobody would stop him. Falau smiled, remembering that Tyler added that the same behavior worked when traveling and when needing to use the restroom in a restaurant you weren't eating at.

Entering the elevator he hit the button for the fourth floor and stood silently with a few students, who smelled of marijuana and did their best not to make eye contact with him. The doors opened and they burst through the opening, not offering to let the older man go first. Falau sighed at the indiscretion and exited the elevator.

Strolling around the mezzanine perimeter of the floor Falau could see that there were students in all areas. A few were complaining about a final they had the next day, shedding light on why the library was so full in the first place.

Coming upon a door marked 'Electrical Closet', he reached for the door, only to find it was locked. However, the pull on the door from Falau's strong arm shattered the silence of the room and caused some of the students to look up at the man trying to enter a closet.

Flashing a quick smile and nodding his head as if to say sorry for the disturbance, his hands searched his pockets for the key. Finding it, he slipped it into the door and turned, as the heads of the students shook with disgust.

Closing the door behind him he quickly took inventory of everything in the small room. A locked circuit breaker. Exposed wire. A tall stool. A thin desk and a pair of pliers left by one of the maintenance men working at the university.

Placing his backpack on the desk he pulled the zipper open to expose the full inside of the pack. At first glance it looked as if the pack was filled with files and student papers. Under the papers were the tools of his trade for the night. A lock picking kit, soldering iron, various cables, clamps, and his 9mm handgun.

Looking at the electrical box he saw that the lock was simple in design and picked up the lock picking kit. Sliding in the two wire strands he slowly felt his way, depressing the areas that would fit the design of the proper key. Bracing the metal strands, he twisted the lock and it popped open without a problem.

"Not bad for the first time in fifteen years," whispered Falau, smiling at the easily completed job.

Looking over the insides of the electrical box he made out wires for basic lights and outlets, but there were also wires for computers and satellite links. The library was fully equipped with state-of-the-art technology at every turn, making life for the students easier.

Pulling open the outside pocket of his back he fished out a small earpiece that was no larger than the tip of a pen and triangular in shape. He slid it into his ear and pulled his cellphone from his pocket. Extracting the number from deep inside his mind he started typing it into the phone, hoping it was right. Tyler refused to let him write it down, even in code, saying it was too valuable.

Without it even ringing Tyler's voice popped up in a happy tone. "Sorry you have missed me, Falau, but that's what I intended in the first place. The recording you're listening to can be played only once. You cannot rewind the information, but you can pause it by pressing pound. So, pay attention and everything will go as smooth as silk."

Falau rubbed his chin with his hand, feeling the unshaved scruff. He hit the pound button, pausing Tyler's words, and laid out his equipment in front of him for easy access, before placing the pack on the floor. Pulling his head close to the door he heard the muttering of students just outside.

Hitting the pound button on the phone again Tyler's voice came back to life. "Your phone is not just a phone, but can function as a laptop computer. I made some adjustments, so you can do everything you need to. Gathering information on our little friend in college is not going to be a problem if you do what you're told. Wise is still considered an enrolled student, so the information on the ID has already been entered into the school's system. They think you're really a teacher there."

Shaking his head at Tyler's ability to go off topic even at a time like this frustrated Falau. He had no idea when someone might come to the door and see what was happening inside. How could he ever convince someone that a professor was in the electrical closet? But Tyler insisted, explaining that people stopped maintenance men to ask for help all the time. Being stand-offish was perfect for a professor in New England.

"Alright. Take the yellow cables I put in the pack and clip one to each lower corner of the phone. Wiggle them into the grooves on the phone and you will hear them click."

Again, Falau hit pound and did as he was told, then reactivated the phone.

"Now look into the electrical box and find a thick wire with telecommunications markings."

Falau could see that all the wires had been labeled inside the electrical box, making his job easier than he'd anticipated.

"Shave off some of the wire's coating and attach the red cable to it."

Following the instructions Falau felt everything was going without a hitch, when suddenly he heard the knob begin to turn on the closet door. Before he could reach out to hold the door shut, it opened to reveal a young Asian man looking in the opposite direction and talking to a friend.

Falau hit pound on the phone and looked at the back of the young man's head. "Can I help you?" he asked, attempting to sound frustrated.

The young man's head spun around and stared at the man with cables rigged up in his hands. "Oh, sorry... bathroom please... no bathroom now," he said, struggling to find the words to a new language and pushing them out in broken English.

Falau smiled at the young man. "No bathroom. Down there. Two doors," said Falau, motioning to the right and holding up two fingers attempting to bridge the language barrier in some easier way.

The young man bowed and moved away from the door with purpose. Falau closed the door as he walked away and went back to his work. Hitting pound again Tyler's voice rang out. "Now, just clip the yellow and the red together, give it about thirty seconds, and the link will be complete. See... it wasn't that hard after all. Mostly because my software is doing all the work, but you had to get in there, so we are even. See ya later. Over and out."

Clipping the cables together the phone screen launched into a frenzy of activity, with numbers and letters crossing the screen. As fast as it had started the screen lit up with a headline that read, "Internal records access accepted." The next line down read, "Student's name:" with a blinking cursor after it.

"Okay, Calvin Wise, let's see what your college career can tell me. Any clues about where you like to go."

Entering the name and pressing GO, full access to the academic history of Calvin Wise appeared on Falau's phone.

"Let's see," Falau mumbled, being sure to keep his voice low so the students outside wouldn't hear him. Clicking on academic records showed poor to fair grades. Two semesters of academic probation. *What's this? One year out of school after his sophomore year for medical reasons?*

Drilling down deeper into the file a series of prompts for passwords popped up, and without having to enter a thing the password was autofilled, leading him to the file containing the reasons for the leave of absence.

Clicking the file to open a scanned document popped up, first from Tridon Psychiatric Department. Written by Dr. Barrett Webber. "Well look at this," he mumbled. *The Patient is diagnosed with intermittent explosive disorder, antisocial personality and a rule out of schizophrenia. It is the recommendation that the student Calvin Wise be sent to an inpatient psychiatric facility for clarification of diagnosis and medical evaluation.* "Interesting."

Scrolling through the records revealed the inpatient record for a five-day stay at the Garden View Psychiatric Hospital. Falau moved to the section listing behavioral issues, where a string of events in his college career were listed and confirmed by Calvin's father. "You were a bad boy, Calvin," whispered Falau. "Kicked out of a fraternity for hazing your second semester freshman year. Four cases of assault before the disciplinary committee. Accused of exposing himself to a female teacher during office hours, causing her to mace him? You are one sick puppy, Calvin. You just can't stop yourself, can you."

Reading deeper into the file Falau found the impressions from the psychiatrist who worked with him, and froze, staring at a single line. "Appears to be responding to internal stimuli."

Reading the line several times before moving on the big man knew exactly what it meant. Calvin was psychotic. Hearing voices or seeing things. The killing was not just for sport, it was part of a condition that was beyond his control. He quietly read on. "The patient has a preoccupation with sexual issues. He continues to expose himself to nurses and has been placed on a one-to-one observation schedule after cornering a nurse in his room and removing his clothing. The patient then demanded she remove her clothing and he would show her true love. During this episode he held his hands in a choking motion as he moved toward her. The nurse screamed, alerting staff who restrained the patient physically and chemically while he was attempting to grab their crotches and breasts."

Scrolling to the bottom of the page Falau read a list of medications that were advised for Calvin Wise to take upon discharge, as well as the name of a therapist and psychiatrist in the community. The final paragraph of the report stared up at Falau, helping him understand the man he was after:

"The Patient has a sense of entitlement fostered from the time of early childhood. Behavioral indiscretions have consistently been handled by the father, with a financial contribution to the school the patient attends. This is true for college, high school, and even grade school. His behavior is unpredictable. He lacks remorse for anything he has done. He is recommended for long-term residential treatment. Patient is refusing all medication and treatment. He is signing himself out of treatment, against all mental advice. Attempt for legal commitment via section 12 made, but declined by judge."

Falau disconnected the phone from the wires and placed all the items back in his backpack. Zipping it up and getting ready to walk out the door, Falau was sure of just one thing; that was Calvin Wise was a far more complicated man than anyone realized.

Chapter 11

For thirteen days Falau ducked in and out of doorways and kept a safe distance from Calvin Wise. Tracking his every move he started to learn the patterns the young killer followed, and was soon anticipating what Wise would do before he'd do it. Keeping precise data, he would trace out the patterns on a map and one glaring problem would rise up again and again. Calvin Wise never spent any time alone outside of his home, and what happened inside the home was unknown to Falau. If he were to successfully take Calvin Wise and get him back to the judges he was going to have to learn more about the inside of the Wise household.

Keeping a low profile, Falau sat across the coffee shop watching Calvin Wise and his father have a donut and a cup of coffee. The coffee shop was not like the big chain stores, with thumping electronic music or plucky little acoustic guitars. This was a mom and pop shop that had retained its location in the financial district of Boston for decades. The ceiling was high with exposed pipes and visible rafters, and the tall glass walls were covered with pockmarks from kicked up stones and high winds over the many years since opening. The tables were small and uncomfortable, with wooden chairs that lacked any padding at all. Along one wall was a bar setup for counter eating that ran half the length of the store, while the other half held display cases with an assortment of donuts and bagels.

Falau had taken the seat at the end of the bar so he could place his back against the wall. He had no fear of the Wise men seeing his face. With any luck, the next time Calvin would see him would be at the moment he was getting captured.

Looking out the window he could see two large men sitting in a Lincoln town car parked on the side of the road. They kept glancing into the coffee shop and watching what Calvin and his father did. Before too long Calvin's father raised a hand and waved to the men, who nodded back in response. Falau now knew that the men were working for Wise and had no problem showing people they were connected.

Across the street two familiar people stood looking across at the coffee shop. One was a beautiful woman covered from head to toe in winter gear that far exceeded the temperature outside. She shivered often, and a grimace would crack across her face with the wind howling down the city streets. The man with her was far more casually dressed. He appeared to be a local, and used to the chill that Boston would deliver within its high winds coming off the water. He held a camera up to his face and was working its zoom back and forth. The camera was clearly professional, and its lens had high telephoto ability, evident by its size. These two had been watching Calvin Wise almost as long as Falau. If not for Falau taking the time to tail them back, he would not know they were reporters for the Boston Tribune online.

The large men in the car kept a sharp eye on the reporters and seemed to hold for them a level of disdain. They would move the car backward and forward to break the line of sight for the photographer, even if it were just for a second or two. But it was far from any kind of chess match between the two sides, more of a ping-pong game between two people that had very little skill in the sport.

Along with all the other patrons of the coffee shop, Falau's head suddenly shot back to the table where Calvin and his father sat, as Calvin's hand hit down hard upon the table and he said in a stern and unrelenting voice, "I am a man, and I will decide what I can and cannot do." Reaching into his pocket he took out a few dollars and dropped them on the table. "I don't need you to pay for me," he barked.

Calvin's father glanced around the room, embarrassed by the scene his son had caused. Leaning forward across the table he spoke in a hushed tone, far too low for Falau to hear what he was saying. Calvin sat back in his chair and nodded, looking down at the ground. His hand reached out, picking up the money and placing it back in his pocket. The two men reached back and started to pull their jackets from the back of their chairs.

Falau stood up and walked toward the door. Timing it just right, Calvin turned and bumped into him as he attempted to go past.

"Watch out, asshole," snipped Calvin giving Falau's body a shove.

Falau stood close, refusing to give an inch to the young man with the brash mouth.

Calvin moved a step closer and looked up, trying to get eye-to-eye with Falau.

"Are you deaf?" he snapped again.

Calvin's father moved in and attempted to split the two men up. As he pushed his hand in between them he told them to "Break it up."

Falau reached slightly forward and slid a small metal object into the thick fabric of Calvin's coat. The object was only slightly larger than a sewing needle and with the same kind of sharp tip. It did its job perfectly, and Falau had flawless execution in the transfer.

Calvin's father turned his son around and pushed him toward the road and out onto the street.

Falau had still not moved from the spot of the confrontation as the two men got into the car with the large men in suits and drove away.

STOPPING THE VAN ONE street away from the Wise home, Falau steered up the street while inspecting the home from afar. The house sat back from the road approximately two-hundred yards. A large stone wall surrounded the property, and there were no trees on the lawn, making the approach to the house extremely difficult.

Pulling out a pair of binoculars to get a better look, he focused on the first floor of the house. A window was open and exposed cabinets along the far wall. Like most homes, the kitchen was at the back of the property, and it was at ground level. Falau knew that if were to find any door unlocked it would be the slider a few feet down from the window he was looking through. Sliders never had self-locking mechanisms in them. It was his best opportunity to get in.

A flash of brown crossed his view of sight, causing a double-take from the big man. He pulled his eyes away from the binoculars and saw several brown objects moving around the back-slider of the house.

Refocusing the binoculars, he opened the field of vision to get a clearer view of the rear of the house.

"Shit!" muttered Falau, realizing what the brown objects were. "Rottweilers!"

Rubbing the sides of his forehead with his index finger and thumb he counted that there were five dogs, all left to their own devices on the lawn. Inspecting them Falau could see that they moved as a group, staying in a pack. If his timing was right he could attempt to avoid them altogether, but if they picked up his scent or heard him they would come as a group and there would be no way to fight them off.

Opening the car door he stepped out onto the street dressed in jeans, a sweatshirt and an overcoat. Stepping onto the sidewalk he slowed his pace so he could take in as much as possible while crossing the street from the house.

He placed in earbuds, as if listening to music, but in fact tuned the frequency to the small microphone he'd earlier slid into Calvin's coat. However, locking in on the location showed no sound at all. Falau's hands ran the receiver through a scan, but nothing connected. The microphone was rendered useless by either an electronic interference from the house, or the microphone was simply broken during Calvin's travels. Regardless of what had happened, Falau was left with no more information than he already had.

Focusing on the driveway, it resembled Tyler's in many ways. It had a bend, and merged with the land leading up to a multi-car garage. A gate at the street boundary would need a special clearance code to get through. The gate looked strong and ready for any impact from a moving car. The wrought iron was ornate, but behind it lie sturdy steel bars.

Walking past the drive the lawn opened up again there was no easy way to approach and get close to the house. The best plan seemed to be throwing caution to the wind and to make a hard move when he felt the time was right.

Turning left at the end of the block Falau lost sight of the house. Going around the block and back to the car was the least obvious way to get there, and knowing that the guards that worked for the Wise family would look at every person and every car that went by made Falau uncomfortable. How good was their intelligence information? Did they use facial recognition? Were they linked into the state of federal government information systems? *There's no way to tell for sure,* he thought.

Arriving back at the car he sat in the driver's seat and started the engine, staring at the house. The only way in would be to go over the wall and to take his chances getting past the dogs. There was just no other way, unless he attempted to go deep cover as a worker. Playing the scenario out in his head he knew that deep cover would mean daytime access into the house. It would mean conversations with people. Most importantly, it would mean limited chances to get Calvin alone and then remove him from the house. Falau figured there were just too many variables to negotiate to make a day time approach realistic.

Pulling open his phone he clicked it to camera mode. Zooming in on the house he took several pictures. Using the binoculars, he helped the camera zoom in to get more detailed shots of the back of the house. Saving the pictures, he uploaded them to a special server that had been left open for him to store his data on. Falau assumed it was government, because Tyler said they were just 'borrowing' space on it.

Walking alongside the main street next to the rock wall that bordered the Wise estate, he spotted two men wearing suits and moving at a quick pace.

No jackets? Falau thought, holding his position to get a better look at the men. *Must be guards who saw me walk by. Probably doing a grounds check.*

The men in the suits were tall, no shorter than six-feet and two-inches. Their shoulders were wide and were filled with muscle, and they appeared to have no neck due to their massive stature. Their suits were well tailored, and the closer they got it became visible that they had on earpieces.

The men cut across the street and started to walk down the middle of the road straight toward Falau in the van. The big man reached down and placed his hand on the gear shift and edged it into drive, never taking his eyes off the two men. If he had to run them down to get away, he would, but it would be a last resort.

While focusing on the two men the driver's side door was suddenly yanked open and a handgun pressed tightly against his head.

"If you move one muscle I will blow your brains all over this car."

Chapter 12

THE COLD HARD STEEL of the gun barrel had a chill to it as it pressed against his temple. The threat to blow his head off made it obvious these men were police or guards. Carjackers would just yank you to the ground and kick you in the face before stealing the car, and a pro sent to take him out would not have said a word. If he were lucky he would have heard the click before the bullet entered his head. But these guys came as a group and talked as if they were from a movie. Amateurs, in more ways than one.

"I'm going to tell you what to do, and you're going to do it," commanded the man holding the gun. "Hands on the top of the steering wheel. Fingers spread apart. No movement, other than what I tell you. Do you understand me?"

Keeping his eyes straight ahead and not so much as blinking, Falau responded to the man. "Crystal clear." His hands slid up the sides of the steering wheel. His fingers spread apart. The two men in suits he'd been watching arrived at the front of the car.

If I punch the gas right now can I get away? he wondered. *I would have to run over the guys in front of me. The quick lurch from the car may get me three feet if I catch the trigger-man off guard. Running over the two guys in the road would slow me down. Even if it didn't slow me down any person with an average shooting ability would be able to hit me before I get away.*

The plan was foolhardy at best, and at worse, suicide. The best plan at this time was to see what these guys had in mind and adjust to whatever the situation dictated.

"Are you armed?" the man demanded.

"Yes."

"What are you carrying?"

"9mm handgun."

A silence fell over the gunman, before he emitted a soft giggle. "I wonder if it's the same one my wife carries."

Unable to help himself, Falau's eyes rolled at the comment and the constant need to point out that his gun wasn't the largest he could have.

"It's just for personal protection," Falau remarked, holding back the sarcasm the best he could.

"With your right hand reach down and put the car in park, then turn off the engine. Do it slowly and methodically. We don't want any problems here."

Falau did as he was told. Applying the brake, he placed his hand on the shift located on the steering column and shoved it into park. Turning the engine off could prove to be a bit trickier. His hand would be obstructed behind the steering column and if the man with the gun got jumpy, he could shoot.

"I'm going to turn it off now," Falau said without turning his head.

"What are you, some kind of smart ass? That's what I told you! Just do it."

Falau followed the instructions to a T. He killed the engine and left the keys in the ignition. He placed his hand back on the top of the steering wheel and spread his fingers. The gunman had not moved the weapon so much as an inch. There was sure to be a pressure mark on his head when the gun was finally removed.

"Reach across your body with your right hand and open the door from the outside. I'm going to step back, but don't take the fact that my gun is not pressed to your head as a sign of weakness. I still have the intense desire to blow your head off. Now begin."

Falau reached across and opened the door, pushing it to its maximum. One leg found its way out onto the ground, soon followed by the next. Keeping his hands in front of him he turned in his seat and pulled himself from the car. It was then he got his first look at the gunman that was ready to end his life at the slightest wrong movement.

The man was unimpressive. He was overweight with a bulbous stomach that hung over his pants, and was barely contained by a white buttoned up shirt. He was the kind of man who might wear suspenders and a belt at the same time. His head was predominantly bald and he used a sad looking comb-over of hair in a failed attempt to conceal it. His face was worn by time and his jowls hung like a basset hound's around his double chin. His look was more of a butcher than a killer. His eyes were a tired brown that lacked the shine of a younger man, but they held an intensity that assured Falau the man was not kidding when he said he would kill him.

The other men, three in total, dressed exactly the same as the gunman. On the sports jacket they all wore was a crest with the words, 'Burnell Security' beneath it.

"Rent-a-cops," Falau said, unable to hold back his feelings.

"Rent-a-cops don't carry guns. We're private security. We have the power to arrest as citizens and defend the property of our boss. Trespassers will be punished accordingly."

"I'm just out here on the street. I don't even know who your boss is."

The gunman walked closer to Falau, holding the gun steady and staring him in the eye. A smile crossed his face, giving Falau a sense that he was not as intense as he first thought. The gunman snapped the handgun hard across Falau's jaw, dropping the big man to his knees. Pulling back his fist clutching the handgun, he slammed his fist down and used the butt of the gun to crack across Falau's nose, breaking it in three places and causing a rapid flow of blood.

"You think I'm fucking with you boy?" barked the lead guard. "You don't think I know you were at the coffee shop, following Calvin for days, then randomly just walked past the house? Do you think we're fools?"

Feeling his nasal passage filling with blood and not being able to focus through his watering eyes, Falau pulled his head back, bobbing in the air like a baby just moments after birth.

Two of the large guards came over. One stood on each side of Falau and placed a hand under his arms, then helped him to a standing position. Their hands were rough and hard, not the kind of guys working security at a gate. They carried themselves like mercenaries Falau had seen in the past.

"You press boys need to learn a lesson about what you can and cannot do. You have no idea who Mr. Wise is, and the power he wields. But you will. You are going to understand everything and make sure other people in the press understand and know their place. And if I see this appear as a story in the paper, then... well, I can promise you nobody will find your body."

The lead guard raised his hand high above his head, exposing the butt of the gun as Falau looked up, unable to defend himself against the on-coming assault. The markings on the bottom of the handle raced at him and cracked against his temple, causing his body to lose the last of its strength. Falau flopped like a rag doll, only stopped from falling to the ground by the hands of the guards that stood by his side. He hung like a slab of meat on a hook, unable even to try to get his feet under him.

"Drop him!" commanded the leader.

Falau's body fell to the ground in a heap, his mind slipping rapidly in and out of consciousness and feelings of intense pain.

The gunman held out his gun, taking aim at Falau's head by staring down the barrel. His jaw tightened and his lips pursed as his finger drifted above the trigger, a whisker away from taking Falau's life.

"Hey boss. He has a camera."

The gunman's concentration was broken by his partner's discovery. His eyes moved to look at the camera being held in the air, and the aim of the gun lost its target of Falau's head.

"Bring it here."

The younger, fitter man came over and handed the camera to his boss.

"Pictures? And what do you need these for?" questioned the leader of the guards. "Can't you people just leave this kid alone? He was found innocent, but you all need to keep following him and his family. No more!!"

He dropped the camera to the ground next to Falau's head and stomped his shoe down hard on it, breaking the lens off the camera. Kicking down over and over again, the camera smashed into a hundred pieces exposing the electronics inside. Reaching down, the leader plucked the SD card from the rubble.

"You're not going to be needing this anymore," he said, tucking it into his inside jacket pocket.

A siren filled the air from the distance though it was unmistakably getting closer. Falau let his body relax, knowing the police would give him some level of protection from the thugs who were insistent on beating him to within an inch of his life.

"Good, police are on the way. Perfect," said the gunman sarcastically as he turned back to Falau, who had now pulled himself to his knees. The gunman smiled and kicked as hard as he could into Falau's stomach. Blood spewed from his mouth as he dropped face down onto the ground. Gravel from the ground decorated his cheeks as he struggled to lift his head.

The police car came to a screeching halt as Falau slowly made it back to his knees. A middle-aged police officer jumped from the car, moving quickly to the leader of the guards. Trying hard to push himself into a standing position Falau fell again as vertigo struck him while trying to find his balance.

"So, this is the guy?" asked the police officer pointing down to Falau. "Get him on his feet."

Two of the guards lifted Falau up, causing extreme nausea, his legs wobbling from the beating he had just taken.

Grabbing Falau's face with his hand the police officer pulled himself in close. "You have a problem with authority, don't you? Well lucky for you I specialize in fixing things like that."

"He broke into the house and attacked the family. He seems like he might be a good candidate for a night time trial with Judge Steinburg," commented the guard leader.

"Consider it done."

The guards gathered their things and started to leave as Falau was pushed into the back of a patrol car by his face.

Sitting in the back of the car Falau looked out the front window and saw the leader of the guards talking with the police officer. Then he handed him an envelope, and Falau realized that a payoff was taking place and it was all about him and whatever the night time trial was. Falau only hoped it wasn't code for being taken out into the country and shot in the head.

Chapter 13

A hand reached out, grabbing him hard by the collar of his shirt, and shoved him forward toward the door of the police station. Trying to resist the shoving Falau bristled, but was easily controlled by the police officer.

Entering into the back door of the police station Falau took notice of all the security cameras. Anyone coming in or out of the station was caught on camera. The building was modern, and an influx of money to the suburbs for municipal improvement projects had resulted in new fire and police stations. The door to bring in a prisoner was far removed from the movies of the past, where a man would be dragged in and banged against the sergeant's desk. Falau was being taken in a door, far out of the public eye, and lower than the ground level at the front of the building.

Banging through the door he noticed the booking area set up for fingerprints and pictures was dead ahead. In the background behind a steel door he could hear the echoed muttering of men and women in cells, spouting off about how they were not the kind of people who should be in there.

Shoving him against the fingerprinting table the police officer leaned up against Falau's back and spoke directly into his ear. "I am going to take your cuffs off now. If you try anything, there are more than fifteen armed police officers on duty tonight. One of us will kill you if you try to run. Is this clear to you?"

"Yes. You will get no problem from me."

"Good."

The key turned and the cuffs popped open. Falau made sure not to move his hands, and left them behind his back, motionless. The officer pulled back.

"Well done. Now place your hands on the fingerprint station."

Falau strictly followed the directions of his captor, making sure not to go astray.

"Why are your fingerprints inconsistent? The patterns have been disrupted," remarked the police officer.

"I'm a metal worker so my hands get cut up a lot."

"So you say. Sometimes career criminals or people with something to hide change their fingerprints."

Falau grunted, dismissing what the officer said as if he had never heard anything so ridiculous. "Can I see a nurse or doctor? I have some bad injuries."

"You should not have attacked them."

"Attacked them? They beat the shit out of me, and I got arrested. I'm shocked you didn't fine me for littering because I bled on the ground!"

"You better not forget who you're dealing with! You keep yapping your mouth you'll get more of what you got on the street. You're screwing with the wrong people. Mr. Wise is a pillar of this community. He built this new station for us. He helps the locals. The trial proved his son was set up and the investigation was faulty. You remember that, and what he can do to you if he wants." The officer banged his fist down hard on Falau's fingers, breaking two against the table.

"AAAAHHHHHH!" screamed Falau, pulling his hand close to his body and hunching over it. "Why?"

"Shut up!"

Grabbing him by the shirt the officer pushed Falau forward, crashing him against the door frame. Pounding his body again, the door triggered open and revealed a bank of cells holding a selection of prisoners. The cells were segregated by sex and ethnicity.

"Looks like you need to make some new friends," said the officer with gritted teeth as he opened a cell with only African-American men in it. "You take your KKK march and shove it," he said, loud enough for all the prisoners to hear, and causing several of the African-American prisoners to turn and inspect their new cell mate.

Chapter 14

FALAU HIT THE FLOOR hard and face first. His battered body struggled hard to fight against the impact, but the cold unforgiving cement of the floor did little to sooth the injuries as his cheek pressed against the harsh ground. His facial wounds reopened and blood started to flow again.

Rolling over Falau's eyes opened, taking in the whole room. Several large African-American men stared down at Falau lying on the ground. Two other men appeared to be passed out on benches, most likely sleeping off drinks from the night before.

A strong, slender black man wearing jeans and a t-shirt tucked into his pants stood up and walked over to the new man lying on the floor.

"So, you're a white supremacist. Always figured you guys were a lot taller."

Falau pulled himself into a sitting position and raised his hand, rubbing the back of it across his cheek. Looking down he could see streaks of blood on his hand, and figured he must be an odd sight for his cell-mates.

Falau's eyes shifted up to the man that now stood over him, looking down with cold, hard eyes.

"You ever hear of a white supremacist that gets beat up by the cops? Especially in a little white town like this?"

The man above him laughed while nodding his head in agreement. "I see what you're driving at, but me and the brothers can't take any chances that we're going to be sharing time with a Klan boy. I'm sure you can understand that."

"Ya. I guess I can understand that. I'm surprised you're going to listen to the blonde-haired, blue-eyed cop that dragged me in here."

Giggling at his own joke Falau looked down at his arm and pulled up his sleeve. Raising his hand up toward the face of the man, he asked, "How many white supremacists or neo-Nazis have olive skin?"

The man grabbed Falau by the arm and inspected it more closely, like a teacher looking for a mistake on an exam paper.

"I would get kicked out of their meetings with skin like this."

Crouching down next to Falau the man dropped his arm. He drew close to Falau and, looking him in the eyes, he smiled. "You make some good points. But we still have the problem that the cops beat your ass and said what they said. How can I let that go? I have a reputation at stake here. Some of these fine men look to me on the street. I can't just let this slip by."

"What will it take for you to believe me. How can I prove that I'm not one of those animals?"

"Well... we could just beat you until you tell us, but my guess is that's what the cops want us to do with you. I have a better idea. You're no kid. What are you, late twenties, early thirties? Ain't no guy I've ever known that's been down with a gang or group that didn't have a tattoo by that age, so he could fly his flag if he had to."

The man stood up, nodding his head at Falau. "Be cool, this will just take a minute and will make everything fine if you're telling the truth."

The man snapped his fingers and the three seated men stood up and approached Falau without hesitation. Two of the men grabbed one arm each and lifted him to his feet in an unceremonious manner.

"Strip him," demanded the leader, looking Falau in the eye and waiting to see if there was any sign of shock or a struggle.

As the men pulled the shirt up over Falau's head and pulled down his pants, he held still, not breaking eye contact with the lead man. As a pair of hands grabbed the -band of his underwear Falau cracked a small smile and then stood completely nude in front of all his cellmates.

"I guess you could call that a dick," said the leader, attempting to be funny but getting no reaction. "You were telling the truth. Sorry for the inconvenience, man. My name's Tips. At least that's what my boys back home call me."

Tips extended his hand and Falau reached out and took it in his own. "Nice to meet you, Tips. My name's Falau. Not to sound disrespectful, but normally someone buys me dinner before taking my clothes off."

"Ya, well what can I say? I move fast. Put your clothes on man."

Falau got dressed in a calm and methodical manner, not wanting his cellmates to think he'd been intimidated by their actions. He still had no idea who they were or what they thought of him.

Tips walked over and sat down with the other men. Waving his hand, he invited Falau to join them on the far side of the cell. Evaluating the cell Falau knew there was no way he could avoid anything. If the men made the choice to take him down he could only fight them off for so long. There was nowhere to retreat to. It was better to make friends with his cellmates and join them, and accept the fact they were all being held in the cell regardless of their skin color.

Sitting down next to Tips Falau looked at the others, who stared back without a word. "Thanks for asking me over," Falau said in a hushed tone.

"You seem cool," replied Tips. "Besides, you're like one of us. Cops beat the shit out of you for nothing. No tattoos at all. No gang, no Aryan nation, not even one for the Red Sox. The only marks on you are the black and blues the boys in blue decorated you with. What did you do to make those boys put such a beating on you?"

"It's a long story, and honestly I'm not sure why they went so nuts on me."

"Well if it's a long story that's good because we don't have nothin' but time in here. It's the weekend and we don't even go to court until Monday, and we will all be good friends by then. So what's the story."

Falau leaned back and glanced at Tips, a small smirk crossing his face. *Could Tips be a plant to get information out of me?* he wondered. *How much should I give up to a person I just met?* Worrying that he'd been given so much slack from his cellmates so quickly made him wonder what their motivation was for wanting to know the story. Maybe it was just to fill the time, but then again, maybe it wasn't.

"Remember that kid on the news that killed that girl? His name is Wise."

"Ya. I remember it. Everyone knew he was guilty but he got away with it. Just like OJ. Money talks."

"I was thinking that I would go over there and check the place out. I took some pictures and hung around for a bit."

Tips sat up straight up in his chair and shook his head at Falau. "You fuckin' nuts boy? You don't go anywhere near that house. Old man

Wise is one of the most connected people around. On the street every-one knows Wise has power and money."

"I know. When I got here I saw they had me down for breaking and en-tering, but I didn't get within two hundred yards of that house. Once the cops got there they put the beating on me and brought me here. Guess they didn't want any resistance."

Holding back the information that the guards had come out and did most of the beating to him gave Falau a moment to read the reaction of Tip's face. Did he know about the guards? His reaction was genuine and plain, as if he were hearing the full story for the first time.

"You need to be very careful about what's going to happen to you next. I got in a fight with the cousin of the Wise kid. Next thing I know three cop cars pulled up to my house and dragged me out. I end up in court with a lawyer telling the judge that I used a bat on the kid and he was in the hospital. They wanted me facing an attempted murder charge. The truth is that I bumped into him at a club and spilled his drink on my shirt! He shoved me, so I punched him. Bunch of dudes jumped in and stopped the whole thing. Next day the cops came. I did three years at county lockup for that shit! Three years for a glancing punch in a night club. Worst thing is they wanted me away for life."

Falau read the lines on Tip's face as he spoke, and the passion in his voice was that of a man who had been done wrong. If he were acting then it was the best performance he had ever seen. When Tips spoke of the Wises there was fear in his eyes and he even glanced around the room to see who was listening. If the street was so well aware of the power and underworld ties that the Wise family had, then the police had to know as well.

"They don't care who they hurt. The father lets the kid kill that girl and who knows how many more, and pays to get him the best legal team in the world," Falau stated, trying to secure his bond with Tips.

"Man, that trial was over before it ever started. The jury the judge and the DA were all in the bag. Everyone knew it. It's only the guys in the press that don't know. And their ain't nobody in the know that will say a word about it. Too risky."

"I'm screwed," said Falau in a hushed tone as Tips nodded his head in agreement.

"Falau! Come on, you're up," said a new police officer as he unlocked the cell door.

"Did I get bailed out?" questioned Falau.

"No. Time for your trial."

"Trial? It's 8:45pm on a Friday night. How can I be having a trial now?"

"Just shut up and get moving," said the officer, grabbing his shirt and pulling him from the cell before he closed the door.

Falau looked back at Tips, who had stood up, his eyes wide. He quickly moved to the door of the cell and reached out his hand.

"Good luck, man. Be safe."

Chapter 15

F alau was ushered hard into the door that led out of the cell block. The guard had little tact, and used Falau as a battering ram to push the door open. With all his knowledge and training Falau instantly felt the police were sloppy for leaving the door open to their cells.

"Get moving, meathead," snapped the guard who had made his feeling for Falau clear by way of a harsh push into the small of his back. The man was enormous, standing six-feet five-inches tall and weighing 270 pounds, though his weight was not that of a fat man. It was muscle from years of working out. The man resembled a large refrigerator with a head, and his level of tact matched just that.

"The door on the right, and make it fast."

Not saying a word Falau stretched out his hand and turned the handle quick to open it. He knew that if he had not kept up the pace walking through the door there would be a clear chance for the guard to strike him again, and this time it may be more than just a push.

The door opened into an ordinary office that lacked sophistication in any form. The room had a large two-way mirror covering one wall, and two metal fold-out chairs in front of a basic desk. On the desk sat a phone, a legal pad, and two sharpened pencils. One office chair on wheels sat behind the desk.

The guard grabbed Falau by the shoulder and pushed down hard. "Sit!" he commanded, making Falau's knees buckle and dropping him hard into the chair. A discernable giggle came from the giant guard as he man-handled Falau. "Hands behind you and through the chair."

Falau did as he had been instructed knowing that any attempt at escaping would be futile. The only way out would be the way he came in. Between him and that door were several officers, all of who were well-armed. It would be like fishing in a barrel for them if he made a run for it.

The guard grabbed at Falau's hands hard, pulling them down and through the opening in the back of the chair. Applying the handcuffs he tightened them to the point they were digging painfully into the wrists of his prisoner. "You just keep your mouth shut and this will all be over soon. But you decide to shoot off your mouth, and you will be giving me all the excuses I need to knock all your teeth out. The boys in prison like newbies with no teeth... understand?"

"Yes," Falau said softly in an attempt to convince the guard he was in a weakened state emotionally, as well as physically.

The door to the office opened without a knock. Another man in a police uniform entered the room, but he had earned stripes on his arm, indicating he was a sergeant on the force.

"Is this the dirt-bag we talked about?" asked the sergeant.

Falau was immediately put off the sergeant just by looking at him. He was a rotund man who lacked any of the physical fitness of his junior officers, his flabby belly hanging low over the belt of his pants. He might convince himself he wore just 40-inch waist pants, but that was just because he wore them so low. His chest sagged and was as fat and droopy as his stomach. His face had thin lips and squinting eyes that wrapped around a bulbous nose. His hair was thin and greasy. Dandruff decorated his shoulders and ears, and he lacked any style or redeemable quality in the eyes of anyone who saw him.

Falau scoffed at the sergeant, attempting to measure him up.

"You got a problem, asshole?" snapped the fat sergeant, spittle flying from his mouth. "I'm sure that little noise that just popped out of you wasn't for me. But just to be clear, if I hear it again we will do this with you unconscious."

Falau nodded, showing that he understood exactly what the sergeant was saying. Floating that trial balloon to assess his reaction let him know clearly this was a man with a low tolerance for behavior he did not want to see, a weak man that ruled his little bit of the world with an iron fist.

Placing a black bag on top of the desk he unzipped the side and pulled out a laptop computer. The sergeant flipped it open and started to boot it up. Taking the bag he placed it on the floor, then stared anxiously at the screen.

The room was silent with just the three of them inside. Falau was sure the other two understood what was happening, but were unwilling to fill him in on the situation. Trying to read the face of the sergeant was impossible. He just stared at the laptop like a monkey trying to figure out a jigsaw puzzle. He had no interest in anything other than doing what he had to do and moving on to the next task. But why was Falau even in the room to begin with?

A voice came from the computer, breaking the silence of the room. "What the hell do you people want with me now?"

"Your Honor, we have a case for you at the request of Mr. Wise," replied the sergeant, suddenly sitting up straight in his seat and adjusting his posture.

"Mr. Wise? Hmmm. Okay. Link him in."

"Yes, Judge Steinburg."

The sergeant went back to typing on the keyboard, pecking out the letters using only his index fingers. A crackling sound came from the speaker on the computer again. "Can you hear me?"

"Yes, Mr. Wise. Your Honor, can you hear Mr. Wise?"

"Yes. Let's get this going. I want to be in bed."

"Yes, Sir. This is the trial of Michael Falau. He is being charged with breaking and entering, assault, and criminal mischief."

Falau rapidly realized that he was being tried now, and not in front of a jury of his own peers. This was a classic backwater railroading, just as was done in small towns where the sheriff, the judge and jailer were all the same man. In the suburbs of Boston maybe they were not the same man, but they took place in the darkness of the night and nobody would be any the wiser.

The fat sergeant belched as he opened his mouth again. "Excuse me. Mr. Wise, do you want to press charges again Michael Falau?"

"Yes, I do. Trash like him cannot be wandering the streets in the commonwealth. Judge, I am sure you will do exactly what is right, as always. By the way, how are Doris and the kids?"

"Very well, and your boy?"

"Great. We're on for golf Saturday morning, so we can catch up more then."

"Just as long as you give me five strokes." An awkward laugh came from both men as if they were a laughter track on a poorly made sitcom.

"We have held you up long enough, Mr. Wise. Please leave the rest of this to us and enjoy the rest of your night," suggested Judge Steinburg to whom appeared to be an old friend.

Mr. Wise hung up his phone with a simple click. No goodbye to the others listening in, who were far below his station in life, and he liked letting them know it with simple acts, such as not saying goodbye.

The sergeant held still for a few moments, building his courage to speak but not wanting to cross in front of the judge in case he wanted to say something. "If it is alright with Judge Steinburg, I would like to ask Mr. Falau how he pleads?"

Falau looked hard into the face of the man with the squinty little eyes. Could he be serious? Is this an actual trial?

"Did you ask how I plead?" asked Falau. "Is this a trial—"

"Oh, shit. I don't need to hear what he pleads," interrupted the judge "It truly doesn't matter what he says."

"Wait!" implored Falau. "Don't I get a lawyer or a phone call? Something? I haven't even had a chance to try to make bail? How can you guys be giving me a trial for something that just happened?"

"It just happened?" questioned the judge. "Sounds like an admission of guilt to me. Thirty days county lockup! Next time don't mess with the children of powerful men." The judge banged something soft against what sounded like a table. No doubt he was attempting to replicate the sound of a gavel.

The link to the judge went dead and all the men in the room said nothing. The sergeant placed his fat hand behind the screen of the laptop and slowly pushed it down until it made a clicking sound, showing it was closed.

"We take everyone having the right to a speedy trial very serious around here," he said, smirking at Falau and attempting to be funny in the face of Falau, who'd just learned he was going to prison.

"This can't hold up. How can this be legal? I should have a lawyer and a real trial. You guys are just making the rules up as you go for the rich guy!" vented Falau.

"I'm going to let you get away with that little rant and not smash your punk-ass face because you're in shock, but if I hear anything more from you it will be beating time. Do you understand?"

Falau nodded, not wanting to infuriate the little troll by speaking.

"Let me give you some advice. You're going to prison at the county. That can be as good or bad as you choose to make it. Do your time and shut up, and you will be out in thirty days. Shoot your mouth off or make a problem, and they will lose your file and you could be there a lot longer. Thirty days is a gift. You think most people with the charges you had would only get thirty days? You would have waited longer than thirty days in lockup just waiting for a trial. You should be happy."

The portly man stood up and stuffed the laptop into the bag from which it came. He walked to the door and opened it. Looking back at Falau, who had not dared turn his head or respond in any way, he smiled.

"You know, it's going to be hard for you in there. Just remember, if you take on one of the big guys as a lover and they will protect you."

Chapter 16

A gray van with a sheriff's department insignia pulled through the gates of the Southern Massachusetts House of Correction as daylight broke over the horizon. The van carried a driver and just one passenger, who sat inside a specially designed cage for transporting prisoners to and from the corrections facility.

Falau looked out sternly between the opening of the metal fencing inside the van. The House of Correction building stood tall and ominous in the morning light. It looked more like an old castle than a prison, and if someone had said it was haunted most would believe it. The building had stood for over a hundred years and despite the modernization and refurbishments inside, it still bore the hard and dark exterior it always had. Stepping through its main doors for a prisoner was like walking into the mouth of a great dragon who was swallowing you whole.

The van door slid open and a burly man in his fifties grunted and motioned for Falau to step from the van. His shackled legs could spread no more than sixteen inches and his hands cuffed together made movement and balance tricky. Grabbing the side of the door of the van he extended his leg, with the tip of his toes just touching the ground.

Getting his feet under him, Falau took a good look around the massive building rising before him. The building extended in each direction for several hundred feet. Windows shone light from night staff that would soon be calling it a day. The facade of the building was stained from years of weather and neglect, and the sooty exhaust from cars. To the sides and beyond the building is where the great wall stood. Not a fence like in the movies, but built from thick stone, mostly the original stones from a hundred years ago, when the prisoners were forced to build the very wall that held them in by using stones from the local quarries. The wall was thirty-feet high with spikes sticking out the top. A razor-sharp barbed wire that rolled around the top was added for good measure. A guard stood in a watchtower every fifty-feet. The silhouettes of two men carrying scoped rifles could easily be seen as the morning sun rose behind them. If one were to try to run from this place these sharp-shooters would have five-hundred yards of open ground to hit their target before they got to the tree line.

"Who the hell did you piss off?" asked a guard who carried no less than forty extra pounds on his modest frame of five-foot, eight inches. His face was round and he wore transition glasses that had started to darken from the rising sun. Under his nose wiggled a bushy mustache that made him look more like a walrus than a man.

"Excuse me?"

"You must have pissed someone off to get a special ride here this early in the morning. Who did you piss off?"

"I got thirty days for a B & E."

The heavy-set guard grunted, amused by what the new prisoner had told him. "Is that what they told you, thirty days?"

"Ya."

"You're not even on record here. You're a special delivery, and I doubt any file will be following you later on. Your time here will be based on what the warden wants to do with you. But I wouldn't go making any dinner plans for the next few months."

"You're joking," said Falau, trying to assess if the portly guard was just trying to scare him.

"Nope. You're fucked."

The guard grabbed Falau by the shoulder and started to guide him into the front door of the beastly prison, though his grip was looser than the other law enforcement he had dealt with. This was a man who knew that Falau had nowhere to go. If Falau did choose to make a break for it, death would meet him swiftly in the form of a bullet in his head.

Stopping at a desk the guard helped Falau down into a chair and then moved himself around to the other side of the desk.

"Okay kid, what's your name?"

"Michael Falau."

"Alright, Mike. I'm the guy that gives everyone orientation around here. I tell them about money getting deposited into an account for the canteen, when visitors can come, and all the other rules. But you're different. You're a special delivery. I have been here over twenty years, and there have only been about a dozen of you. You must have pissed off the wrong person at the wrong time. You're not going to get any canteen or visitors. The system will not list you as existing, or you're going to be put in by another name. Most guys in your situation don't get out of here alive. The other prisoners take care of that. The best thing you can do is stay low and don't interact with anyone. Then just hope for the best. That's all I got for ya, kid."

The burly guard slapped his hand on the desk and stood up. Within seconds a younger guard came through the door. Muscles rippled through his short sleeve shirt, stretching the material to its fullest extent. His hair was cut into a flat top and he looked to be the same height as Falau. His immediate disposition was harsh and militaristic. He stood at attention and waited for an order from the hefty guard.

"Shit, Jimmy, enough with the attention stuff. You're not in the Marines anymore. This guy is Falau... take him for processing and onto cell block G. The orders are strict with him. No adjustments."

The young guard grabbed Falau by the shirt, pulling him up and out of the chair. "You heard the man, time to move on. Let's go," barked the rambunctious guard.

Falau gained his feet again and shuffled to the door as the young guard yelled at him to move faster. Looking back over his shoulder the older guard gave him an affirming nod and a clenched fist, indicating that he needed to stay strong. Falau knew that the old timer had been around the block a time or two and he wasn't just blowing sunshine up his skirt. He was letting him know what to expect and how to get out of this place alive. He knew that being off the grid in a place like this meant death, if that's what they wanted. Another inmate could kill him over a simple rumor, and nobody would be the wiser.

Heading into a door that read 'issued clothing', Falau's foot hit the frame of the door, causing him to fall to the ground in a heap, unable to brace himself due to being handcuffed. He slapped hard against the tile floor. He grunted as blood started to flow again as his cheek smacked hard on the floor. The day had produced a beating on Falau that was not hidden to anyone, and he was not at all upset by it. The words of Grady rang in his ears... *too pretty for prison.* Looking at the pool of blood forming around his face, he was sure that was not the case anymore.

The brash young guard's foot suddenly found its way firmly into Falau's mid-section, causing him to gasp for air. "What the hell are you doing lying down, prisoner? Does this look like a place of rest to you?"

With the little strength Falau had left, he managed to roll his eyes. The young guard acted like he was in a movie about boot camp, himself playing the part of the drill instructor. Falau knew it was just best to ride the wave of his exuberance and move on to the next thing, but a deep desire to punch him leaked into the back of his mind.

"You understand all this now and your life here will be easier," commanded the young guard. "You will do everything I say. You will do it when I say to do it. If you do not do what I say, then I will beat you until you understand. I am your God. I am your life. Without me you have nothing. Do I make myself clear?"

Pulling himself from the floor and with blood running down the side of his, face Falau nodded.

"I said, do I make myself clear?" demanded the young man, looking for Falau to subjugate himself to the power he held over him.

"Yes."

"I have a few questions for you, and you will answer them with honesty. If you lie you will never get out of here. You will die in this godforsaken hell-hole."

Attempting to stand up as straight as he could Falau held his tongue from telling the guard he was laying it on a bit thick. Falau smiled to himself, realizing maybe he was maturing, and finally able to control the smart-ass side of his personality.

"Be careful how you answer the following questions. Your life depends on it," said the guard, reducing his volume to a normal tone. "Why were you at Mr. Wise's house?"

"I was there to get pictures."

"Who were you working for?"

"Freelance."

"Who wants pictures of Mr. Wise?"

"Nobody wants pictures of him, they want them of his son. Every paper and online blog will pay top dollar for pics of him."

"When you say top dollar, how much are we talking about?"

"A standard picture on the street, about $100. Get him at home with a telephoto lens and it rises to about $500. But the big one is him on a computer or coming out of a bar. Then get you a minimum of $1000. I figured from the location I was in, if I was lucky I could get a few of him in the house."

"You were wrong," snapped the guard, clearly disgusted with the line of work Falau was feeding him. The guard paused, trying to read his face. "What camera do you use?"

"Nikon."

"Model number?"

"D810."

"Film?"

"None. Digital."

The guard hit him with rapid-fire questions, looking for a weakness in his story, but Falau provided none. He was sure the guard would not have the discipline to go back later to check what he'd said was right. He was only looking for a physical change in Falau or for him to crack.

"Okay, I'm done with you." The guard reached to his shoulder, depressing the hand microphone that rested there. "Trash to be taken out to Cell Block G."

"Coming to pick up the trash," responded a voice from the other end of the communication device.

"Be careful in there," mocked the guard, pointing his finger at Falau and wiggling it in a childlike motion. "Those guys are not very friendly when it comes to outsiders moving into their little community. If you think I'm bad just wait and see what they have in store for you."

Chapter 17

———

Falau was led through the corridors of the large prison, often needing to stop and wait for an automatic door to open between one section of the facility to another. It was a constant maze of hallways that led to foyers of every office and cell block. The only thing that could open them was central control, or the eye in the sky, as the inmates called it. They had control of all the doors and they could lock the entire prison down with the flick of a switch. If a riot were to break out one had better pray they were on the right side of the doors, or they would be locked in with the rioters themselves. Containment was the prison's best friend.

Falau learned quick—as he was pushed against the wall—that prisoners kept to the side and walked on a yellow line that ran on each side of the hallway. Down the center was a blue strip that was for personnel and visitors. If a member of the personnel or visitors needed to get by, a guard would call out "coming through" and all the inmates would stop walking and immediately face the wall, not permitted to look back to see who was going by. Once the person passed then the inmates would again go on their way.

"Stop here," commanded the guard as they reached a large door on the right with the letter G visible in massive print. The guard pressed a small button next to the door and waited without making any conversation with Falau.

The door opened after a few moments and he ushered Falau into a small area. The door closed behind them. This foyer area led back the way they came to the hallway, but on the other side Falau could see into the cell block. The guard again pressed the button and waited without saying a word. The large steel door started to slide to the right, unveiling all of cellblock G.

"Your home," mocked the guard, pushing Falau through the door into the block. The door slowly slid closed behind him and the loud click of the lock coursed through his body and mind. Now, more than any time before, he realized he was to be caged like an animal. He was in the domain of another man who would decide when and how he should do things. He was a prisoner in every sense of the word.

The cell block was cold and hard. Despite housing more than forty men it was spotless from top to bottom. The ceiling was high, about forty-feet, and the room was approximately fifty-yards across. The middle was wide open and scattered with plastic chairs and sofas that were bolted to the ground. Along the back wall was a large double door that led out to a caged-in recreation area with a basketball hoop.

The cells were set on two tiers. The first level was on the ground floor and steps led up to the second level in four places, two at the front and two at the back. The cell doors were solid steel with a small window for the prisoner to look out or another to look in. In the middle of the door was a large mail slot that locked from the outside, and was used to pass books or to unlock prisoners from handcuffs from outside the cell while they were still inside. All this was monitored by a guard station, from where in-block security took place.

The guard from the station stepped down from his post and walked over to Falau. He was a tall and slender man who carried none of the arrogance he was becoming accustomed to in the jail. When he spoke a southern accent filled the air, and he bore a quiet confidence about him, yet felt no need to show it.

"New guy, huh," he said to Falau and the guard.

"He is your problem now. Orders are cell G238."

"Well, okay. Sounds like you're someone who's on the radar of some big people."

The guard that led Falau to the cell block went back the way he came, leaving Falau in his new home.

"I'm going to undo these cuffs. Be smart, or you will have to wear them forever. Now face against the wall."

Falau did as instructed without saying a word. He could see that the guard was skilled at his job. He removed the cuffs without putting himself into a position to be attacked. He controlled the area without being aggressive or attacking. He was smooth and confident in his skills.

Turning around on the command of the guard Falau's wrists were released in the same fashion, and now he stood face to face with a guard in the cell block that would hold him for who knew how long.

The men in the cells started to stir. Falau could hear them yelling and chanting at him. Over and over he heard men call, "Fish! Fish!" and "Ripe! Ripe!" Attempting to ignore it, Falau looked to the ground and then up at the guard who stared at him, standing motionless.

"I know you can hear that," he said in a calm and measured voice. "Fish means you're a new fish in the pond and they are getting ready to go fishing. See if they can break you. The ripe thing means you're ripe for the picking. They want to pull you off the tree of life and have you for themselves. Basically, there is going to be a race to see who can make you their bitch first."

Falau's eye did not blink while listening to the man. He felt himself tensing up and realized he would need to fall back on all the training he had ever had to handle this situation.

The guard smiled at Falau before continuing. "Now, you can try to be a badass and fight everyone in here, but that's a long shot. You could make a big splash and try to scare everyone off, but that's also a long shot. Or, you could just be someone's bitch and they will protect you from the others. Honestly, the only thing that gets any respect in here is the system of who owns who."

Nodding his head indicating he understood, Falau still remained silent, but now with a hardened expression on his face.

"I need to take you to your cell to meet your new roommate. You're not going to be happy. Sorry."

The guard pointed Falau towards the closest set of steps that led up to the second floor. The two made their way to the far end of the room to the stairs. At the top of the steps they went to the center cell on that level. Of all the cells on the block, this cell would take the longest to reach if there was a need to help someone.

Falau looked through the opening of the door to see a man sleeping in a bed on the bottom bunk. He was motionless and seemed at peace. The cell was small, approximately ten-feet by ten-feet. It contained two beds stacked in bunk bed fashion, a desk, and a combination toilet with sink attached to the top.

"Mr. Falau, could you please step aside so I can introduce you to your new roommate."

The guard grasped his communicator on his shoulder and called to the main security for the cell to be opened, and within moments the door started to slide open.

"What the fuck, it's not even seven yet," squawked the big man lying in the bed with a thick Mexican accent.

"Sorry, but you have a new roommate," responded the guard in a polite voice. Wake up was only five more minutes, so all doors would be open soon anyway.

"Another fucking roommate! When will you people learn that I don't like roommates!"

The man in the bed rolled onto his back and put his feet to the floor. With all the skill and agility of a cat he popped up and consumed the center of the small cell. His boots were still on his feet and looked to be military. He wore long pants that were prison issue. His bare chest was stacked with muscle that rippled with each movement he made. Standing six-foot, six-inches, tall he weighed in at 265 pounds. His hands were enormous and covered with scars. He was adorned with a large tattoo of a crucifix cross on his chest and a rosary on his back. Two scars dug in deep and hard to his face. Clearly, they had been untreated and left to heal on their own. Long, jet-black hair hung below his shoulders, the color matching the small beard on his chin that reached up to a thick mustache beneath a strong nose.

"Mr. Falau, this is Mr. Santos. He has lived in this cell for around ten years. He has not done well with cell mates, but I think you two might just hit it off."

"Fuck him!" snapped Santos, pointing at Falau. "I don't want any fucking gringo in here with me."

"Mr. Santos, we have talked about this before. You got put in a prison in Massachusetts. All we have is gringos."

Santos grunted and pulled his shoulders back, making an audible crack in an attempt to intimidate the newcomer.

"Now Mr. Santos, I need to let you know that Mr. Falau is not much of a conversationalist. In fact, I have not even heard him say one word yet.

I think that he will be smart and not get in your way. Then he can just sleep in the cell at night and be out for the day. Is that okay with you?"

"No! But it sounds like I have no choice," replied Santos, almost sounding reasonable "I will have my single room back soon. You can count on that!"

"No threats, Mr. Santos. We don't need to be doing ten minute checks on you again, do we?"

"No. I couldn't even take a shit without you all looking in on me last time you did that."

"Then don't kill people, and we won't do it. You see, Mr. Falau, Mr. Santos came to us after killing three people in El Paso, Texas in the drug wars along the border. He is with us for life. Since being here for almost ten years, he has made it his sport to kill people, eleven in total since coming to us. If he were still in Texas they would have given him the chair by now."

"But I am not in Texas. No death penalty here. I am in for life, so why not kill? What can you do to me? Nothing!"

"Well, I'm sure you two will get along just fine."

"Another snitch. They always send me the snitches."

"I didn't say that, Mr. Santos! And that's not true."

A loud buzzer rang out and the sound of all the cell doors sliding open filled the quiet.

Falau stood motionless, looking in at Santos who stared back without moving an inch.

Chapter 18

S antos stood in the middle of the cell, not giving Falau an inch of leeway. He hardened his body and dug himself in as the other inmates started to walk out of their cells to inspect what was going on. They knew not to get too close to Santos' cell. He had a reputation for getting angry at the slightest thing and resorting to violence immediately.

Falau stared in at the big man, fixing his eyes on Santos and showing no weakness. It was a delicate situation. The wrong move here would lead to an impossible situation, and Falau was looking to keep things as smooth as possible and fly under the radar. Causing a disruption would be the worst thing that could happen and would land him in prison longer than he could imagine.

"So your name is Santos?" Falau said, trying to convey confidence in his voice.

Santos just grunted and gritted his teeth. His chest and arms tightened as he flexed his muscles. Intimidation came easy to the big man, and he had a look that would back most men off. But he wasn't dealing with just any man.

"Santos, it's not like you or I have a choice. I have to live in this cell with you."

"Fuck you!"

Falau surveyed the man and looked for a weakness. He had scars all over but they all seemed to be from fights rather than a surgery. No weak bones that could be targeted once a fight started. One thing was clear... Santos wasn't going to take the change in his living situation in his stride.

"Okay, big man, I'm coming in."

Falau drew in a deep breath and readied himself for the fight of his life. Close-quarters combat with a physical wonder. After the recent heavy beating Falau had taken, this would be an all-out war for him.

Falau walked calmly and directly into the cell, going chest to chest with Santos, who still did not move an inch.

"Excuse me, Mr. Santos. May I get by you?"

Santos started to breathe hard through his nose and his chest heaved up and down. It was becoming more and more apparent he would rather use intimidation to get Falau to leave than physical violence. The big man slowly turned to the side and let Falau by.

Making his way to the back of the cell Falau kept himself face to face with his cellmate when he was edging past him. There was barely enough room for the two of them to pass each other with the beds so close. Moving to the back of the cell he turned on the faucets to the sink and washed his hands and face, waiting to see if Santos made a move.

The sound of rollers caught Falau's ear. Turning back to the center of the room, he saw that Santos had closed the cell door about three-quarters of the way and had resumed his spot in the middle of the room, standing hard and strong.

Falau wiped his hands on his shirt and leaned back against the sink. "So, is this where you kill me?"

"No."

"Then why close the door?"

"You now belong to me. You are my property. You will do whatever I tell you to do, or you will die."

"Doesn't sound like much of a deal to me. Sounds like you get all the benefits, and I end up running around for you as an errand boy," Falau said with confidence. He straightened up and took a step closer to Santos. "Maybe we can strike a better deal than that. How about we live nicely together and nobody dies?"

"Who do you think you are? You have been here twenty minutes and you think you can start to dictate what happens?" Santos reached his hand down under the bottom bunk, and came up holding a makeshift knife. The shank had been made from a sharpened spoon with a large wad of duct tape for a handle. He turned his wrist in a twisting motion, pointing it at Falau. He then jammed it hard into the desk, leaving it sticking straight up.

"Nice shank," Falau said, knowing Santos was ready for the confrontation. This would be the moment were Falau would live or die, become independent or another man's bitch.

"Time for you to prove you belong to me." Santos raised his hand and brushed it across Falau's cheek, running it over the corner of his mouth. "You will now get on your knees and show me how badly you want to live."

"You want me to beg?" questioned Falau, knowing that that was not at all what the big Mexican man wanted.

"No, you are going to give me a blowjob. You are now my woman. On your knees!" Santos grabbed Falau by the shoulders and pushed him to the ground.

Falau did not put up much of a fight and dropped, with his face at waist height of the powerful man.

"If you do not make me happy, this shank will be stuck in your ear and I will twist it until your brains run out like liquid."

Falau kneeled, motionless on the floor. He noticed that nobody was coming near the door. No inmates and no guards. This kind of thing must have been standard behavior for a new inmate to go through.

Santos left the shank stuck into the desk. He reached for the drawstring on his orange state issued pants, his thick, hardened hands fumbling to undo the knot.

Falau looked up at him with a blank expression on his face, and Santos returned the eye contact as his pants dropped to the ground, revealing all of himself to Falau.

"Tonight I will bend you over the desk. This is now your life," said Santos, flashing a yellow nicotine stained smile, the scars on his face becoming more jagged. "Time to do your job and show me why I want to keep you around. If everything goes well I will have you branded as mine within a week. Now open your mouth."

The Mexican pushed his hips forward into Falau's face, getting close but not touching. Falau knew that Santos wanted him to come to him to commit the act. Falau would have to willingly give himself over to the big man. It was a simple yet ultimately controlling move that would gain him more power within the prison system. Other inmates would crack just by his reputation and intimidation. It had always worked before, so why should this time be any different?

Falau glanced back up to Santos who continued to look down at him. Opening his mouth Falau started to move closer, and Santos leaned his head back waiting to be pleasured.

Suddenly, and pulling with as much force as he could, Falau yanked hard on the pants that were still wrapped around Santos' ankles. His feet flew out from beneath him and he fell, hitting down hard on his back and head onto the concrete floor. Falau was sure that with all of his injuries there was no way he could beat Santos in a standard fight, so he attacked in the dirtiest way he could.

If Santos wanted Falau touching his genitals, that was exactly what he would get. Falau pushed himself forward, lying on the pants that now pinned Santos' legs down. With two hands he reached out and grabbed the Mexican by his testicles and squeezed as hard as he could.

Santos let out a roar of pain as Falau attempted to crush the man in his hands. He punched down on Falau but only hit the back of his head and breaking his index finger in the process. The big man felt as if he was starting to choke.

Grasping tighter still, Falau pulled with all he had to drag Santos closer to him. Each time the big man raised a hand to strike him Falau ducked his head and rolled his balls in his hands.

Feeling his testicles laying one on top of the other the newcomer squeezed his fist, creating a feeling like the crushing of a plum, breaking away the soft outer tissue and leaving just the hard stone behind.

Santos' arms flayed in pain and he could muster no voice to scream. His eyes rolled back into his head. He reached out to Falau, looking down and seeing the new cellmate changing position so he looked like a rower in a boat, his full body facing Santos. His feet pressed into the killer's thighs as he sat down, leaning forward with two hands still wrapped around the manhood of the mad Mexican.

"Now you're going to open your mouth for me," snapped Falau as he leaned back with force, digging his feet into Santos and pulling as hard as he could. As he leaned back he stretched the man as far as he could, but then he felt his body drop a little further back, and then a little more. Santos was tearing.

Falau knew he could stop now and the point would be made. But he felt something overcoming him. It was not anger or hate. He didn't know quite what it was, but he somehow knew he was not going to stop. This feeling had overcome him before, in rare situations where his primal instincts took control and he found himself engaged in things that he would never normally do. At times like this he was sure he was losing himself to something bigger, more powerful than him. And yet regret never followed his possessed actions, and that's what scared him the most.

Falau gave another mighty rip, and he flopped back hard against the floor, holding the scrotum and testicles of the man he'd just met minutes before.

Santos laid back on the floor, passed out from the extreme pain and shock, his mouth gaping open.

Falau tossed the contents of his hands into the sink and grabbed the shank from the table. Not hesitating a moment, he started to use the shank to cut away at the man's penis. Falau knew this was extreme, but he needed to send a message to everyone in the cell block that he was off limits. Besides, this was kill or be killed. If Santos were to live through this he should count himself lucky. It was clear he would have killed Falau if he had made up his mind to do so.

Tossing the penis into the sink next to its long-time partners, Falau pulled the big Mexican up into a sitting position, blood flowing from his crotch at a steady pace.

"This is crazy," Falau said, then taking the penis, testicles and scrotum from the sink and stuffing them into Santos' own mouth.

Falau looked himself over and saw no blood on his clothing. He had positioned himself carefully to avoid that. He took his time to wash his hands and wipe down anything with his prints on it.

Calmly, he stepped over Santos' body and opened the cell door and walked out. Calmly walking along the platform of the second floor he could feel all eyes on him. He went down the stairs and sat down at the TV with several other inmates, who were all staring at him without saying a word. He made no eye contact with anyone.

A commotion suddenly shattered the silence from the second tier.

"Guards, quick! Santos looks dead!" yelled a skinny African-American man pointing back into the cell where Santos lay in a pool of his own blood.

The other inmates all looked at Falau, who let a wry smile curl his lips for just a second.

Chapter 19

TERRELL WILKS RAN BY the name T-Bone on the streets of Boston. He was a big fish in a little pond, meaning his gang was small but he was the leader.

Black Boston 617, or BB617, was well known despite having only thirty members. They were up and comers, known to run their small spot of turf with power and aggression. Anyone caught dealing on one of their streets would be shot on sight, whether day or night. The streets around Ruggles Transit stop belonged to them, approximately a half-mile in all directions other than the college Northeastern that was on the other side of the track. They knew to stay clear of the college kids. Nothing would cause the police to come down harder than some lily-white college kid getting zapped in the subway.

With a gang so small it was hard to hand out assignments to lower level guys. There just were not that many bodies to go around, and recruiting was job one, so that's where most of the manpower was going. T-bone preferred to lead by example. Stepping up and doing jobs himself made it impossible for other guys to say no when asked to do the same thing. In another gang, leadership never played a street role, but this was T-bone, a man known for pulling his own trigger and pushing his own supply of smack. It was said that he liked the risk, and enjoyed dancing with death.

A scarred face and battered body were the results of loving that danger. He wore his leadership on his body like badges of courage. He was not exactly disfigured, but one needed to tell themselves to not stare at him when they met.

In his younger days he had a standoff with a rival gang member who looked at his already deeply scarred face and told him, "You look like ashes and smell like smoke."

T-bone reacted in a rage and ended up burning the young man after beating him senseless. Rumors spread throughout the years that he just may have been from ashes and smoke, because no matter what anyone did to him he would not die. He had been shot, stabbed, and run over, but he always came back and would later burn the people responsible for attacking him.

Now he stood in a prison yard holding his own little piece of turf. Only himself and two other inmates were from BB617, and there was no way they could compete with the Bloods, Crips, Latin Kings or MS13. Their numbers were just too great. Besides, the big gangs didn't worry about the small timers. They saw them as drone bees working for the bigger gangs, and they didn't care about their vibrato as long as they brought back the money from the drugs sold and the special assignments given to them.

A toothpick sat in the corner of his mouth as he leaned against a twenty-foot high chain-link fence, just one of the many barriers to get through if someone attempted to escape. Taking a breath, he lifted his hands to his mouth, blowing out and warming them as he watched the newcomer Falau strolling about the yard as if he did not have a care in the world. The guy who cut off and jammed Santos junk into his mouth and got away with it. The guy who caused Santos to attempt suicide when he was told he was going back to the same cell block as Falau. The guy who was in the prison as a special delivery like him.

Two years earlier T-Bone saw BB617 on the verge of rapid expansion. They were just at thirty members, up from twenty a month before. Kids on the street were seeking them out and wanted to know how to join. BB617 had killed a police officer during a drive-by shooting of a rival gang's home. The story got embellished by the kids on the street, who said that T-bone walked up to the officer and shot him in the face and then lit him on fire. It was a great story for the angry kids to focus on, and BB617 was not about to change the story that was helping them gain a ton of street credit.

The truth was far more simple. T-bone led three others in a drive-by of a rival gang member who lived just one street over from their turf. The kid ran with the South Side Possy, made up of six members. His name was Ramon and he had a habit of drifting up into the BB617 territory to sell his junk. He liked to dance both sides of the street that defined where BB617 had control. He was brash, and attempted to instigate with the larger and more successful gang.

T-Bone saw this as a potential opportunity to recruit the SSP and make them members of the BB617. To him it seemed like a win-win situation for everyone. Ramon would get better protection and could sell anywhere in the area, and BB617 got more members. The problem was, Ramon didn't see it that way, and declared war on T-bone and the BB617.

Six months later T-Bone stood on a street corner and was selling a small bag of heroin to a college kid, who crossed the tracks to get his fix, when a 2012 Ford Taurus raced up the street with two-gun men hanging out the passenger side windows. As they hit the corner, T-bone saw them coming. He smiled at the mistake that they didn't wait to show themselves till the last second. He dove behind the car that got rattled with bullets streaming from a shotgun and an Uzi.

One of the bullets found its way into his right arm. Rolling over to stand, he could see the college boy standing perfectly still where he had been before the transaction. He was shaking and silent. T-bone stood up. "You okay man?'

But nothing came from the boy.

Police sirens filled the air and T-bone made a run for it. Looking back over his shoulder he could see the boy still not moving, paralyzed by the shock of what had happened. With a bullet in his arm he made his way to a doorway he knew was unlocked and looked down the street, seeing the police arrive at the boy.

Later that night, after trying to remove the bullet from his arm for hours by using hospital forceps and gin to pour on the wound, he gave up and went to the hospital. The ER doctor removed the bullet quickly, but the police arrived just as he finished, insisting they would take T-bone in for questioning.

T-bone was a direct admission to the House of Correction. The kid buying the drugs was the son of a close personal friend of Mr. Wise. T-Bone wasn't even given the hope of the telephonic trial or a trip to the local precinct. He just went to jail, knowing nobody would know or care if he was there. If anyone snooped around too much they could just kill him, and nobody would ever know. Just as Falau had been told, it was better for him to keep a low profile and shut up.

A smile drifted across T-bone's face, watching people avoid Falau as he walked toward them. They were literally clearing a path for him. Just one month after almost killing a man and doing unspeakable things to him, every inmate and guard thought he was insane. Nobody dared cross the man that would rip your nuts off and feed them to you. The more time went by the more the story got embellished. Going from dismemberment and a ram into the mouth, to Falau spoon feeding him his manhood while he was still conscious. All of this was greatly increased because the mystery man spoke to nobody and nobody spoke to him. He walked in silence and would randomly smile or mutter to himself.

"Must be the voices in his head. Who is he talking to?" questioned one of the inmates.

"Maybe the fucking voices told him to do it. It's just a matter of time before he does it again. I had a cousin like that and when he got the taste for killing he kept going," spouted off another inmate.

T-Bone didn't believe any of it. He watched, and examined how he always walked the same pattern around the yard. How he always ate at the same seat in the mess hall. How he would always take the same spot in line. He was a creature of habit. He liked things a certain way. He liked them predictable and steady. He liked things set in a way that he could control. And with just one insane action of ripping off another man's genitalia, he had gained just that; control of the people around him, the environment, and how he was treated. The guy was smart and cagey. Crazy like a fox. He knew what he was doing and who he was doing it to, and if need be he would do it again in order to control things.

This was the guy that could help, thought T-bone. *He can be the one that gets out of this place and can make some waves for the rest of us. There are some debts to be settled, and this guy has the mind, skill and attitude to overtake and destroy the biggest, meanest and most aggressive inmate on cell block G. If Santos couldn't take him out or even leave a scratch mark on him, then who could? Not a guard or another inmate.*

Falau turned at the edge of the yard and started making his way toward T-bone. He had a good fifty yards to go before the two would be face to face. T-bone made his assessment of the possibly insane killer and he was sure Falau had also made an assessment of him. The stakes were as high as they could be. If he stopped Falau or walked with him, and Falau was indeed insane, he would probably attack him and rip a chunk of his body off.

But if he was right, and the man was more tactical than insane...

Well, then he would have just made the best friend he could have in the entire prison.

Chapter 20

FALAU WATCHED AS THE black man stepped out from his spot along the fence and squared himself up in the pathway. He was in no way a large man, but his confidence shone through like a flashlight piercing the dark.

The man wore orange prison pants like the rest of the inmates and on his top half was a denim jacket with orange stripes down the sleeves. A wool cap sat on his head and he flicked a toothpick in his mouth as his head sat cocked to the side.

Falau knew he was being measured up by the man he'd observed every day in both the TV area and yard. They called him T-Bone, a small-time gang leader who lived just a short distance from Falau's apartment. Of all the people to step up and challenge him, it was surprising it was this man. He had little backing in the joint, so if things went bad for him with Falau there would be nobody to jump in and help him.

Choosing not to break either his stride or his direction, Falau calculated that the low-level gangster would choose to risk his life fighting the man who now had the entire prison backing away from him. Moving closer and closer he could see the hardness in T-Bone's eyes. He wasn't breaking eye contact, and when he'd reached within ten feet T-Bone tilted his head, and said, "Sup?"

Falau stopped in in his tracks, stared at the gang member, and didn't say a word. He tightened his eyes and gritted his teeth behind his lips.

All eyes in the yard turned to the men in their sudden standoff, and an audible buzz went from person to person, spreading the news that a standoff was actually happening.

The guards outside the first fence and in the towers had shifted their attention to the two men. If they were to fight one-on-one, then the ground guards would stop it. If it were to turn into a riot then the tower guards would be ready to fire if a guard on the ground got into trouble.

T-bone smiled and nodded his head again. "Sup?"

"Not much," grunted Falau, unwilling to show he was impressed with the man for his guts and determination.

"Mind if I walk with you?"

"Do whatever you want."

"Good."

T-bone turned to the side, opening the path for Falau, and joined him as he walked by. Falau watched his movements and examined T-bone, looking for his angle with the walk.

The different groups, men that gathered by gang affiliation around the yard, watched the two making their way around the outdoor area. Immediately, all the groups wondered if T-bone was making a play to get Falau as a new member, or at least have good relations with the man they all felt was insane.

"I hear your name is Falau," T-bone said, nervously starting a conversation.

"Ya."

"What is that, Mexican?"

"What do you want?"

A devilish grin crossed T-Bone's face and he wasn't afraid to show it. "You don't beat around the bush, do you Mr. Falau. No casual chit-chat for you."

"You out here walking with me for exercise, then fine, we can keep walking. But if you're out here for anything else then get to it," snapped Falau, giving no quarter in his prison personality.

"Just relax, man. I'm not here for any trouble. I like my balls right where they are."

The casual quip caught Falau off guard, and a swift smile crossed his face before he rapidly dismissed it and dropped into character.

"Ya! I saw that. There is a little human inside there."

"What do you want, convict?"

"Okay, but I will get you to laugh," said T-Bone in the most disarming way he could. "I think you and I could help each other out."

"No."

"What do you mean, no? You haven't even heard what I have to say," T-bone replied, looking both confused and outraged. He was not used to the total lack of respect. There was a certain way things were done in prison, and Falau was not following prison culture. He was brash and aggressive, and all without a reason. "Listen to me, man. You need friends in here whether you like it or not."

"I'll take my chances."

"Then you're going to end up dead in here. If not by some young punk who wants to kill the guy who dropped Santos, then it will be old age. Either way, your last days will be spent in this shit hole."

"I'm going to do my time and walk out of this place. That's it."

Stopping and placing his hands on his hips, T-Bone shook his head. "You think you have a release date from here?"

Falau kept moving and T-bone moved quickly alongside him. "Release dates are for formal prisoners, not guys like us."

Falau's head tilted and looked over to the man walking beside him. "What do you mean, like us?"

"I mean, guys who got stuck in here from that mother fucker Wise."

Falau's face contorted as he processed the words he'd just heard.

"Ya, that's right, you're not the only one in here because of him. There are four of us in total. They try to keep us away from each other by putting us in different cell blocks. Someone screwed up and put you with me."

"What does it matter? We'll get out at some point."

T-bone started shaking his head and looking at the ground. "Come on, man, you're smarter than that. Why would they ever let us go? They don't need us talking about what happened to us. They don't want us going to the press. They don't want us taking revenge."

The word revenge dug deep into Falau's mind. The sentence was truer than anything he had ever heard, yet he had not acknowledged it before this moment. Of course they would never let him go, because he could return and attack Wise and his family. It was better to leave him in prison and let him rot.

"How can they do that?" asked Falau, now with less defiance in his voice. "They can't just leave us here."

"Man, it's been happening since the beginning of time. If you have power you can remove your enemies. Just get rid of them by killing them or sending them away. It's just the way it happens in Boston, like everywhere else in the world. Same shit, different city."

Falau knew the man was right, and realized that prison life was now a permanent possibility.

"You didn't think that they just let that situation with you and Santos go by without doing anything? You do that to a man, even in prison, there are charges and more time added to your sentence. But you're a ghost in here. You don't exist on the records, so nothing happened. You were never going to get out anyway."

"You're from Boston?" asked Falau, changing the subject rapidly so he could buy time to process the information.

"Ya."

"What part?"

"A block or two off Massachusetts Avenue on Columbus Avenue going outbound."

"Down near Ruggles T?"

"You know the area?"

"I live a few blocks over in one of the old brownstones on Massachusetts Avenue. Guess we're neighbors."

"The brownstones. My uncle Grady lives over there."

Falau stopped short and raised his head to T-bone for the first time. "Grady's your uncle?"

"You know him?"

"You could say that. We've shared a few stories and many drinks over the last few years."

Falau started walking again feeling a growing kinship with T-bone, though his darker side began questioning if the kid had done his research and was just playing to Falau's emotional side and weakening him up for something sinister.

"I can get you out," said T-bone, plainly and without emotion.

"The hell you can. If you could get me out you'd be long gone yourself."

"Ya, you would think that, but the problem is I got nowhere to go. My family and friends are all in a two-block section of town. I can't take off and leave them all to make a new life somewhere."

"Isn't it worth a shot if you've found a way to get out?"

"Man, I have the system down to a science. It's easier than you think, but what happens when I get to the outside? I don't have the skills or money to be on the run. They would find me in a week."

Falau glanced over at his walking partner. "What makes you think I could do any better."

"Come on, man. Everyone here knows the way you handled Santos was not just the actions of some goofball fighter from the street. You walked out without a scratch on you. That is some serious secret agent stuff, or at least top-shelf military. Hell, normal people can't do something like that and then walk down and watch TV."

"I'm just a regular guy," Falau said with a smirk.

"If you're a regular guy then I'm the leader of the Klan. You have what it takes to get out of here... and then you can do me a favor."

"A favor?"

"Ya, a favor. I'm not going to give you a present this big without you doing something for me."

"I'm listening."

"I'm not going to ask you to kill, or ask for money. Nothing like that. I just want you to expose Wise and what he's doing. Drop a dime to the press."

Falau nodded his head in agreement. "Thought you inmates hated snitches?"

"This isn't snitching. It's revenge. I wish I could have you kill the son of a bitch and his murdering son, but the authorities will catch up to you if that happens."

"Let me think about it."

"You want to think about it? A chance to get out of here? It's a chance to be free again, and all I want you to do is call a newspaper and bust the same guy that stuck you in here. What the hell more do you want?" questioned T-bone, his voice getting louder.

"There's just one problem?"

"What's that?" asked T-bone.

"I don't trust you."

T-bone stopped in his tracks, as Falau continued, walking calmly away.

Chapter 21

Sitting down on the floor with his back against the wall Falau kept to himself. Twenty yards away the other inmates gathered around a TV watching football and cheering for the team of their choice. Falau didn't even attempt to see the score or watch a replay.

The inmates and guards left the man with the vicious reputation alone, because nobody wanted to meet the same fate as Santos. Most felt that it would have been better for the huge Mexican to die rather than live his life castrated like a bull that was no longer needed to breed. Word in the prison was, Santos had fallen into a deep depression, and it didn't seem like he was going to come out of it. He was placed on a continuous suicide watch and spent almost all his time in the psychiatric unit.

T-bone had been keeping his distance and had not re-engaged Falau over the last week. Falau admired his patience, and knew the gang leader was playing the situation to perfection. Falau would obviously keep thinking about the offer, and when he came back to talk about it then T-bone would be ready for him.

Falau inspected T-bone from afar. He observed his interactions and the way he handled people. He wasn't trained by an expert, and had learned his trade on the street. The man could read people, and had a knack of telling people the things they wanted to hear. He had the ability to make a man do just the thing he wanted him to do, but the man would think it was his own idea and not T-bone's. He was a salesman through and through, only the things he sold to guys on the street were drugs and the dream of a better life.

A loud groan came from the inmates watching the football game. Falau assumed it has been a score for the team they were against, but the men hushed down and a news bulletin came across the screen, saying, 'Breaking News', and an attractive blonde woman appeared on the screen.

"We're sorry to interrupt your regularly scheduled shows at this time. A fifth body has been found in the last two weeks, this time in a motel on Route 18 in Weymouth. It looks to again be the work of the Loving Killer. We now go live to Chet Sermon in Weymouth. Chet."

The inmates all shifted their attention firmly on the screen. The guards would normally turn off any programing that could anger the inmates, and football was about the most intense thing they were allowed to watch. If there were problems on the cell block, even that would be taken away as well. But today the guard wasn't paying attention and was letting the men enjoy the game without interfering. He now had no idea what they were watching.

"Thank you, Lisa," said the handsome young man, his slicked-back blonde hair an effort to make himself look older than he really was. "The Loving Killer has done it again. This time his victim was found in a Weymouth motel. The situation appears the same as the other murder, with a young woman left nude in bed, strangled but not sexually assaulted. Just a few months ago Calvin Wise was tried for a similar murder and found not guilty. Police now fear that the real killer is back at it, and possible copycat killers are involved."

The screen flashed to show a picture of a young black woman dressed in what looked like a prom gown and smiling at the camera. The young man in a tuxedo next to her had his face blurred out. The reporter continued. "Just moments ago Police Chief Rex Childs gave us the name of the victim, a Shauna Washington of Dorchester."

"What?!" shouted a slender man sat next to T-bone. "Shauna?"

Falau recognized the guy as T-bone's right-hand man. He would run messages for T-bone and play the go-between when gangs interacted. The man was smart and a skillful speaker. He could mend bridges in an environment where people were often just killed, no questions asked.

The man stood up on his chair and reached for the screen, trying to touch the picture of the murdered woman. A tear rolled down his cheek.

"Hey, off the chair!" yelled the guard, using the control to shut down the TV.

"No! Turn it back on! That's Shauna! He killed Shauna!"

"I said get off the chair... Now!" barked the guard using the overhead speaker.

Other inmates pleaded with the man to get down as his crying became more intense. He could not or would not hear them. Overcome with grief, he struggled to form his words.

"She's my cousin," he sputtered between gasps of air that had overcome him with his crying.

"No!" he shouted, staring at the ceiling and pleading with God to change what he'd just seen.

The large door to the cell block slowly slid open and several guards in riot gear entered the room. They moved toward the distraught man on the chair.

"Hey man, there's no need for this. The dude just learned that his cousin was killed. He's just upset!" yelled T-bone, trying to alert the guards to the situation.

The guards moved forward in unison like a well-oiled machine. They were in lock step and ready for anything the inmates may throw at them. "Stand down, inmate," yelled one of the heavily armored guards.

"She was my cousin! They killed her! They killed her! Why?" shouted the heartbroken man, still not moving from his position. "Please, turn it back on. I need to help her. I want to see her face."

"GET DOWN NOW!" screamed the most advanced officer while pointing his night stick at his target.

T-bone stepped forward, raising his hands and attempting to settle the situation. "Sir, I can get him down. Just let me ta—"

A night-stick slid through the air, striking hard into T-bone's kidney. One of the guards off to the side did not like his approach and dropped him to the ground with one swift and well placed blow. Raising his stick again he slammed another blow across T-bone's back, dropping him flat to his stomach and moaning in pain.

"Any of you other inmates want to try and step up?" the big guard said, kicking T-bone aside.

The inmates backed off slowly, but not without jeers and comments pleading the guards to take it easy on their cell mate.

The guards were not so inclined to take such chances with their own safety. Making the demand to step down from the chair one last time, the man looked to them covered in tears.

"What if it were your cousin?" he questioned, looking for compassion.

The main guard reached up and grabbed his shirt and pulled him down from the chair as the other guards took him to the ground. In moments they had him cuffed at the ankles and wrists. Carrying him like a tied hog, they had him out of the cell block in less than two minutes.

T-bone still lay on the ground, attempting to get himself together. The pain shot through his shoulders and kidney with every move he made. The other inmates steered clear of any injured man, unwilling to offend his pride by offering help. T-Bone was no exception to this. He was proud, and one of his own had just been attacked.

Falau pulled himself out of his sitting position and leaned against the wall as he watched T-bone get back to his feet and take a few deep breaths. He watched T-Bone holding his back where the nightstick had hit. He knew that the guards had to be aggressive and had to take control of all situations, but he still felt an anger about this one. It lacked any compassion for T-bone or the man who'd just learned a family member had been killed.

Falau had heard just enough to know that Calvin Wise was up to his old tricks again, but now he had a license to kill. His father made sure of that. The only change was, he was looking for girls from the hood, and not young white girls from the local colleges. He didn't even have the modesty to change the way he was killing them. He was thumbing his nose at everyone, knowing they could not stop him.

Something had to be done about Calvin Wise, and it wasn't going to happen with him sitting in a jail cell.

The judges had obviously not put another person on the case, he thought. *Were they waiting for him to get out to continue the mission?* He knew that the judges based their work on patience, so it was possible they didn't care if they got their man now or in a year's time, just as long as they got their man.

Lifting his head, T-Bone locked eyes with Falau. The gang leader flashed him a solid smile. "Just a bump," he joked, but he lost all humor as he grunted hard in the middle of his words. A grimace flashed across his face as he sat down in the same hard-backed chair his gang mate had just been pulled down from. The other inmates watched as Falau and T-Bone sized each other up again. Nobody moved as Falau's face remained void of emotion.

"What you looking at, man?" questioned T-Bone. "If you got something to say just say it. If not then stop giving me those psycho killer eyes of yours," he snapped, no longer afraid of cell block G's biggest badass.

Falau pulled himself from the wall and slowly approached T-bone, the other inmates now fixated on the collision that was about to happen. Would they really get to see what Falau could do in person? How far would he get before the guards were back and dragging him away?

Falau approached T-bone without hesitation and stopped directly in front of him, and looked down without dropping his head.

"What, Falau? What do you have to say to me?" questioned T-bone with both attitude and anger from the beating he'd just taken.

"I'm in," said Falau softly before he walked away.

Chapter 22

Tossing a small rubber ball into the air, attempting to get it as close to the ceiling as possible without hitting it, seemed like a reasonable way to spend a morning when all you had was time.

Time is the enemy of all inmates. People on the outside talk about how time flies and how quick their kids grow up. *My god,* they say, *where have all the years gone?* But prison time is slow time... slow and hard. It marches on, but defies the laws of the universe and takes longer for each second, minute, day and year. A man can dramatically age by years in a matter of days.

The lifestyle consists of being constantly on edge and ready for a fight. Soldiers get a break from battle and are sent for rest and relaxation in order to calm them from the perils of war and the heightened senses they have to carry at all times. Prisoners get no such break. They carry that level of alertness until they snap, and have a problem with another inmate, a guard or, often, with themselves. Then they get sent to solitary, where there's nothing to stimulate them, no contact with anyone or anything. That rapid change can transform a weak person into a wreck, begging to be brought back to their cell in tears.

For Falau the cell was no place of happiness. Tossing the ball up did pass the time but his mind was fertile and alive with thought. He did everything he could to occupy his mind. He studied the walls and counted the marks on the ceiling. He gave himself projects, like cleaning and exercising, but it did nothing to calm his racing mind.

Filling his day caused him to drift along to the cell block's daily meeting for Alcoholics Anonymous. He never did get the courage to go in, but he heard men talking about the big book and Bill W. He wanted to go in, but also knew that any sign of weakness would be something other prisoners would pounce on. The group or medical care would have been an easier route to take through detox in the first two weeks he was there, because the cold turkey he'd subjected himself to was a painful and dangerous way to get sober.

The memories and the flashbacks had become more intense with sobriety and the infinite time to think. They filled his mind every night, and the worry of them coming on was just as bad as the images themselves.

Her face jumping into his sight. Almost never the beautiful and gentle face of love, but rather the blood-covered mask of a woman who had the life knocked out of her.

She whispered to him throughout the day: "You killed me. It's your fault. You like to kill. You like causing pain."

He longed for the whiskey to fight off images of Santos' body slumped on the ground, with his genitalia ripped from him and stuffed into his mouth. Those images would often flash before his eyes. He could still see blood stains on the floor every time he walked into the cell.

She questioned him: "Why did you do that to him? You didn't have to, right?"

And she was right. Something took him over as it had in the past, and he was then capable of acts that later filled him with shame and regret. But which character was the real him?

"Knock Knock, man," called out T-bone, now standing in the doorway of the cell.

Falau caught the ball and shifted his eyes to T-bone, who wore the smile of a man who had just gotten what he wanted.

"What the hell are you smiling at?" mocked Falau.

"Oh, I had a feeling that you'd come around. It's only so long that a man can stay in this place without the overwhelming need to get the hell out."

"True. Helps that everyone is starting to size me up again. The fear of what happened to Santos is starting to fade."

"There are short memories in the joint when it comes to shit like that. It's all about whose ass have you kicked lately."

Falau chuckled as he sat up in bed. "So, I guess you have a plan for what you want to do?"

"Ya, I have a plan, but I have to talk to you about something first."

"Come inside and sit down. Too many ears out there ready to rat anyone out."

T-bone slid in the doorway and pulled it halfway closed. He knew eyes would already be watching the cell to see if Falau would repeat the Santos incident. Time was short to do what needed to be done.

"I had a visitor yesterday," said T-bone firmly.

Falau's eyes darted to his friend and locked on his with hard determination. His mind raced with questions.

"A visitor? How?"

"I know... nobody knows I'm in here. A guard I've never seen approached me and said I needed to go with him."

"You've never seen the guard? We don't have anyone new on the block."

"So the guy takes me to the visitor area. The place is hopping with people. He tells me that my attorney is there to see me and that I need to sit down at the open booth."

Falau lowered his feet to the floor, focusing on what T-bone had to say. Despite the friendship he'd forged with him he still watched the man for any signs that he was lying, or just hanging around him for information. That observation skill was beyond his control. It was as if he was on auto-pilot and all the information around him was assessed and broken down. It was now a mode of survival more than anything else.

"This dude sits down. Sharp dressed white guy, looking like he just came out of a GQ spread. He just sits there and looks at me."

"Did he say anything?" questioned Falau, wondering if T-bone had been compromised by someone who right now was gaining information on who he was and what he was doing.

"Here's the thing. He said next to nothing. He just looked at me and told me to tell you to believe me."

Falau suddenly felt T-bone had tipped his hand with a sloppy cover for what he wanted Falau to do. He was being set up by the gang leader, who would gain control of the cell block, at least for a short time, by getting Falau busted. Falau knew that he couldn't show any sign of recognition that he'd sniffed out what T-Bone was up to.

"He did say one more thing," added T-bone with a quizzical look on his face. "He said to tell you his name is Tyler. Then he got up and walked away."

Falau's eyes widened uncontrollably. There was no way T-bone knew of Tyler. He could not have just pulled that name out of thin air. Tyler had visited him, and T-bone passed the message on in exactly the way Tyler had intended. It was exactly what Falau needed to ensure he could trust T-bone and his plan. As usual, Tyler had made the right move at just the right time.

Chapter 23

T-Bone reached behind himself and pulled his shirt up over his pants. Glancing out the half-open door he checked to see if anyone was coming. The coast was clear, and he removed the tightly wrapped flat package and tossed it onto the bed next to Falau.

"It's time," said T-bone, as cold and hard as an ice storm.

"Time for what?" asked Falau, looking quickly at his friend.

"Time for you to get out."

"Now?" questioned Falau, overcome with the information. His mind grappled the information, trying to figure out how it was possible to escape from prison at 10:30 in in the morning. There had been no elaborate plan or system of escape. T-bone had never even spoken with him about what steps they'd need to ensure he wouldn't get caught. There was no way he could be expected to memorize and complete a task as large as a prison escape in just moments.

"Open the package. There's a new uniform in there for you."

Falau ripped at the package like a child on Christmas morning and found another prison uniform. *Why would I need a new uniform?* he thought to himself.

"This is my escape. A new prison uniform?"

"And a new identification number and name. Your new name is Albert Raize. You were arrested for OUI nine months ago, but you have a perfect behavior record, not even a mark for speaking out of turn on your sheet. Today's the day you get released."

Falau nodded his head slightly, thinking of the simplicity of the plan and how it was perfect by being so basic. He would walk out the front door, the guards showing him the way.

"What happened to the real Albert Raize?" Falau asked, unable to stop himself.

"Albert is going to do one more month with us. In a month's time he'll take the place of another guy who isn't going to make it."

"Why did he agree to that?

"Albert had a problem betting on football. Thought he could beat the point spread. He was in the hole to me for $20,000 when he got busted. If he did this for me the debt gets forgiven. If he disagreed then my rates as a loan shark would have him paying his debt forever."

"And the other guy who won't make it?"

"He has problems with the Kings. He took some dope from them, but used it rather than selling it. They want to whack him now, but I convinced them it'd be better to watch him dry out in prison and then take him out the day before his release date. Albert will just slide into his spot."

Falau held the new uniform in his hands and looked at the new serial number. His escape involved a death, just like every other thing in his life.

In the back of his mind a soft voice called with an echo. "It's your fault. You killed me."

Quashing the voice the best he could the big man turned all his attention back to T-Bone.

"Will Albert dummy up?"

"Ya, Albert is no problem. He has a wife and kids. If he opens his mouth about all this he believes we'll kill his family. Not the kind of thing I do, but it works to get these degenerate gamblers to pay back their debts. It's always the white dudes from the suburbs that think they know more about sports than Vegas."

Standing up Falau walked over to his desk and reached under it, pulling out a small bag. He turned back around to his friend and tossed the bag to him.

"It's my stash. A thank you present. Not a lot, but things you can use. A shank, two packs of cigarettes, some weed and a good sized bag of heroin. Stuff that should be good for trading. Just my small way to say thanks."

"All the thanks I need is fucking up Wise. You blow the show on him and that whack-job kid of his with no loose ends and we all end up happy."

"When do you get out?"

"Never. Unless Wise takes off then I'm stuck right here. It's the only way I can make sure my family is okay," T-bone said, standing up and placing one hand on the door to show he was ready to make his move to leave. He tucked the stash from Falau into his pants and smiled. "Listen close. They're going to take us to chow in a few minutes. That's when they'll come to pull Albert from the line. When they call the name you walk out and go with the guards. Simple as that."

Falau knew his friend was right. It was simple, though a million things could still go wrong with the plan. But doing it in plain sight with all eyes on him was better than sneaking through a tunnel in the middle of the night.

"Thanks man," said Falau, sticking out his hand for T-Bone to shake.

The gang leader looked at Falau. "Normally people hug at a time like this, but we're in the joint and a hug leaves you wide open for attack. Mr. Falau, I have no idea if you're a very good man or a very bad man, but I'm damn happy you're my friend." T-bone reached out and shook hands, realizing that the two men had never touched in all the time Falau had been in the prison. They were both far too cautious to themselves vulnerable to attack.

The buzzer sounded, indicating they needed to line up for chow. T-bone left the cell and hustled to his spot on the floor as Falau slid on the new uniform. He looked at the dust and grime on the material. T-bone had made sure to get the uniform into a worn out state. The only difference between this uniform and his own was the identification number across the right breast pocket and running down the leg of the pants.

Just like every other meal time, Falau followed protocol and went down and took his spot in line. He waited for the automatic doors to open, and all prisoners went out the doors into the hallway single-file to join the other members of cell block H who were right across the hall.

A young guard walked between the two lines as they started to move to go to chow.

"Raize. Albert Raize."

Falau stepped out of line and in front of the guard. He smiled, assuming the look of a man about to get released from prison.

"Let me check your number, Raize. 9-2-6-1-1-2-1-5-8. Okay, come with me. Time for you to get out of here."

"Yes sir," said Falau, walking with purpose behind the guard. The sense of formality had dropped, the guard making him walk to the side. A free man in waiting was given a bit more liberty on his way out the door.

The guard unlocked the door with the words OUTGOING PRO-CESSING written on it. As the door opened Falau was shocked with the level of activity he saw in the room. Over a dozen men were getting processed to leave the prison that day. The room was only the size of a high school classroom, but the walls had openings and counters, just like the DMV. Each window had its own purpose. Paperwork, personal items, cash, transportation, and parole assignments.

"Sit here and wait to be called for each window. When you're done at the window sit back down and they will process you at the next. Good Luck."

Falau took his place on the long row of benches and thought of all the ways that the escape could go wrong at this point. There had to be a picture of Raize in the file. What if someone saw it and noticed he was clearly not the man who should be leaving the prison? Could he fight his way out? Doubtful, what with the number of armed guards and the wall that would still need to be scaled.

"Raize, Albert!" shouted a man sitting in the 'Parole' window. Coming face to face with the man Falau noticed it was the same man who had originally taken him from the van when he arrived in the wee hours of the morning. The man flashed a smile his way and sat up straight in his chair.

"Well, look who it is," he said with a devilish grin. "Isn't this interesting."

Falau looked at the man, searching for the right words, but nothing came to mind. He stammered a little, then simply nodded his head.

"Son, you're getting a second chance out there, so don't blow it," said the older guard pointing his finger at Falau. "Funny I was here the day you came and now the day you leave. What got you in here in the first place?"

"Being stupid and drunk. I have a problem with drinking. I need to get into some groups and get my life together."

"You're damn right with that. Only thing that will work. I've gone twenty six years without a drop of alcohol. Not even at weddings. Getting sober saved my life and kept me from losing my wife and kids. No matter what you do, get yourself sober. It's hard to start with but after a while you begin to deal with all the things you were drinking about in the first place."

Despite the guard having no idea he was talking to the wrong man, his words rang true for Falau and his own life. He struggled to deal with the truth of life and his past. Maybe being sober was the way to do it, but to this point the bottle was the only thing that had ever helped him.

"Yes sir. I know it will be a long road to get to the right place."

"Now that's what I like to here. Now, you need to check in with your parole officer twice a week," said the older guy while sliding a piece of paper across the counter. "You do that and stay sober, and you'll be all set. Best of luck young man."

"I will, sir. You seem like a fine man, but I hope I never see you again." Falau and the man chuckled at the simple joke.

Falau returned to his seat and waited to be called to the next window and the next until he had finished.

After receiving his personal effects, or at least the ones that belonged to Albert Raize, he slipped into the jeans and T-shirt. He checked the wallet and found $3.

The man behind the counter smiled at him and passed him a bus ticket and $50 cash. "Best of luck. You can now walk out that door to freedom."

Falau held his breath for a second, then gathered his things. He passed through the first glass doors and walked the long hallway to another set of glass doors. He kept thinking to himself that T-Bone was in the wrong kind of work. He was a tactician. Most people would never escape in such a simple way. They would make it unnecessarily difficult for themselves. But T-Bone spotted a weakness in their system and focused on it and created a plan. He had deliberately sprung it on Falau with no time to waste, just so he wouldn't think about it too much. He was smooth and skilled. If he did get out of this rat-infested trap, he would be a good contact to have on the street.

He reached down and pushed the lever of the glass doors, opening up onto the outside world for the first time in months. He stepped out into the cold, late winter air and felt a shiver. He didn't have a coat. The bus stop was across the street. Looking to the right and getting ready to cross, a black Mercedes sped up to him and stopped on a dime. The window dropped down to reveal Tyler, a wide smile on his face. He was listening to the song 'Chain Gang' by Sam Cooke.

"Need a ride, convict?" he asked with a wink.

Chapter 24

Opening the door of the luxury sports car, Falau smiled. The small car seat would feel more comfortable for his body than anything in the prison had in months.

"How was your vacation?" asked Tyler as he stepped on the gas and pulled away from the curb.

"Relaxing, but the people next door just made way too much noise," said Falau, in an exasperated tone.

"Well I hope you didn't fill up on sweets because I got you a treat," responded Tyler, reaching between the seats and pulling up a brown paper. "I thought, if I were in prison for a few months what would I want to have first? So I got you a cheeseburger and fries."

Falau tore into the bag and pulled out the two cheeseburgers wrapped in their familiar yellow paper. He dropped the fries into the bag and stuffed a few into his mouth.

"Mmmm. What, no shake?"

"Sorry, but I didn't know what flavor you liked best. We can stop for one."

Falau laughed and took a large bite from the cheeseburger, enjoying every morsel of the unhealthy but sorely missed food.

"Wow, you're doing a number on that burger."

"It's been a long time. Hey, how did you know to talk with T-Bone?"

"Did you forget?"

"Forget what?"

"We know everything. Once we did our investigation we knew where you were within forty-eight hours. We ran background on everyone in the cell block. T-Bone stuck out like a sore thumb."

"Was he just a mark, or did you think he could help in the future?"

"Hold on, Falau, you're not part of recruiting. If he gets out you tell him nothing. If he can give you information fine, but it ends there. Nothing more. He has too many connections to the area to do what we do. Is that clear?"

"Ya, it's perfectly clear. Just a question, man. Don't worry, he knows nothing. He's a sharp guy so he knew not to question anything about you even after he met you."

Tyler looked straight ahead and kept his eyes on the road, fighting back a grin.

Falau looked at his friend, waiting for him to break the silence, but all he did was drop the visor to stop the sun from shining into his eyes.

"You didn't meet with him, did you."

"What do you think? Why would I open myself up to that? I had a friend take care of that for me. We look a lot alike, so if your jail friend described him to you it was close enough to sound like me."

"Never anything out of place for you is there?"

Tyler shifted his eyes to his friend and a serious look spread across his face. "I try to make sure there isn't anything out of place. If there is, I'm the guy who has to fix it. Better to have it right the first time than to do it twice. No mistakes, then nobody dies."

Falau heard him loud and clear. Tyler was the straw that stirred the drink. He was the one that everything revolved around. There was no way to tell how many cases he was working on all around the world, how many people put their lives in his hands. But through all of it, here he was picking up his friend and making him feel as if he was the only person he had to deal with.

"Sorry, man. I didn't mean to sound like I was mocking you at all. Prison messes with your thinking and you say things a bit different. I will square away."

"I understand. It can mess with you."

"Have you done time?" questioned Falau, turning in his chair and taking another big bite of the burger.

"That's a story for another day. Let's get our eyes on the prize."

Chapter 25

Tyler was driving as hard as he always did, foot hard on the gas and weaving in and out of traffic without a care in the world. It was his special way of making sure nobody was following him.

"Some things never change," said Falau, grinning at his old friend and holding on to the bar above the passenger side window. "If it works, might as well stay with it." Falau shifted comfortably in the seat, enjoying the luxury of being inside the car. "What happened to the Dodge?"

"Oh, your old love machine? Well I have her ready for you. The moment those guys picked you up and we got word of it, we had a team out there grabbing the car, your coat, and all your other things. Oh, by the way... I have this for you." Tyler reached inside his jacket to his chest pocket, removing a 9mm handgun. A Ruger SR9C, to be exact. He handed the weapon to Falau and smiled. "I think you're old friends with this."

Falau chuckled and took the gun in his hand. He pulled back the slide to see if there was a bullet in the chamber and saw that there was. He slid the gun down behind his back and shoved it into his jeans. Suddenly he felt more comfortable being armed and having some means of defense.

Tyler looked at Falau as he hammered down on the gas and entered the highway at top speed. The car moved with grace and precision as the exits flew quickly by. "Okay, listen carefully. This is the situation. You're still on the job. You're the man that needs to bring in Calvin Wise. That assignment didn't just disappear when you went into prison. In fact it got more pronounced. I'm sure you heard and saw some of the news inside. More girls have fallen victim to the exact same crime he committed. From the intelligence we have he's certainly the guy doing it, but the police are simply turning a blind eye to it. There's even talk of the FBI coming in to bust this little prick. But as of right now nobody from federal has come in. Seems like his old man has too much control over everybody around here."

"No problem. I'm glad to see the work is still there. Needless to say I need the money and this will be a good start for me. Just let me get back home and put myself together. In a few days I'll be back on the case."

"Sorry buddy. That's not going to happen this time. We need you on the case right now. If you can't do it we need to get somebody else."

"Tyler, I'm not asking for much. I'm just asking for a chance to get back home and pull myself together, develop a new plan and get focused on what needs to be done."

"I understand your concern. But our concern is that this kid is a killing machine. He doesn't let up. He doesn't stop. He just keeps killing. Are you able to take on this mission and continue it now?"

Falau reached down to the bag to pull out some more fries but there were none left. "I see how it is... first you butter a guy up with a cheeseburger and french fries, and then you lower the boom on them," said Falau, laughing and placing his hand on the shoulder of his friend.

"You're not answering the question."

"Okay, I'm in. Take me to the Dodge, let me get behind that class act of a car, and I'll be ready to roll."

Chapter 26

Tyler's car came to a screeching halt outside of a Suburban garage that looked more like a storage unit than anything else. Shifting slightly in the seat he opened the car's center console, retrieving papers, pens and a wad of cash.

Shuffling through the different items he came across a card inside a sleeve that was no bigger than a credit card.

"Falau, here's the key to get you through the gate, and it'll also get you into the garage. Go to the one marked A-275. Pass the card over the sensor and you're in. The Dodge will be in there, so pull it out. The door will close automatically behind you, then you're on your way to do the job. I don't need the card later, so just throw it away or destroy it."

"Sounds simple enough. Take care, my friend."

Falau opened the door to the car and stepped out onto the sidewalk. He calmly walked into the storage area and soon heard Tyler's fast car ripping away. He smiled, thinking perhaps Tyler did not know how to drive in a calm and sane fashion.

Approaching to the locker he passed the card in front of it, just as he had been told, and the door automatically rose. The ugly red Dodge 2000 Caravan sat there in all its glory, just as he remembered it. Falau hopped inside and found the keys in the ignition. Glancing down at the buttons, they remained the same, and still had all the deadly force the Tyler had informed him about before. On the passenger seat sat the coat, sunglasses, and a box of the new bullets Tyler had made just for his 9mm.

The key turned and the engine came to life with a sputter. There was a high-pitched whine, almost like the fan was out of sync and creating some disruption. Falau was sure Tyler had even developed this feature to make the car fit the profile all the more.

Outside the storage complex Falau steered the car down the road in the most casual of fashions. He wanted to blend in with all the other soccer moms and dads who were ready for their kids to take the field in the most gentle and non-contact ways.

If only Tyler were here, the two of us together could take care of this and it would be no problem, though Falau while scratching his chin. But that wasn't to be. Tyler indicated clearly and often that he did not get involved with that part of the mission, and his important work was somewhere else.

Within twenty minutes Falau pulled up to the same spot he'd been months before with a clear view of the Wise home. Looking out he saw the rolling landscape that went up to the house and the wall that defended it. He used the binoculars to check down the street to the gate and then up again to the garage that sat on the hill. Minimal activity, and nothing to see. Scanning the grounds with a binocular every five to ten minutes, nothing appeared to change. The Rottweilers came out for their runs, combing the area and running in a pack. They still proved to be the biggest problem in his mind. They were obviously well trained, and defended their territory to keep any intruders away from the Wise home.

With the binoculars still in place Falau spotted two men coming out from the gate on the street. They were dressed in the same suits the men had worn months earlier when he had been arrested. These men, however, were younger, fitter, and had a stronger look of determination.

Their jackets flapped in the breeze, and Falau could clearly make out each one of them had a shoulder holster that contained a handgun. These guards of the Wise home gave no indication that they were out for anything other than to get to Falau in the van, so Falau wasted no time, and turned the engine over and started the car again. He knew these men would hold him until the police arrived, just as the others had done before. He would probably get a good beating for being there a second time, and God knows what they would do to him to make sure it wouldn't happen a third.

The men hustled directly across the street in a diagonal direction toward Falau.

Falau dropped the car into gear and sped from the curb, the wheels gripping the street hard. He went straight toward the two men, playing a game of chicken and knowing there was no way they could win. The two men froze in their tracks and reached for their guns. Falau hammered the gas hard, surging the car right at them. As the distance closed, the men realized there was no hope of opening fire on Falau on the streets and bailed off to the sides as he drove past them and made a hard right at the corner and driving away from the Wise home.

Looking in the rearview mirror he could see one of the guards talking into his shoulder radio, probably alerting the other guards in the home that he had made a break for it. His only hope now was to gain some distance from them and be able to slip away.

Taking another sharp turn to the right and then the first left, Falau found himself moving into the countryside, and a large open stretch of road where he was able to edge past the speed limit and not get himself pulled over by the police.

As the big man rolled along, frequently checking his rearview mirror, he started to feel at ease that the guards were not in pursuit.

Chapter 27

F alau rode the gas hard, taking another right and then a quick left. After a series of twists and turns he got the car onto an open road and was soon passing by large fields. It had to have been fifteen minutes, and the men were nowhere to be seen. Falau reached over to his jacket on the passenger seat and felt inside the chest pocket. He'd been dying for a smoke, and after the tension with the guards it was exactly what he needed to calm himself down. Digging into the pocket he realized the cigarettes were gone. Tyler had managed to give him all the things that he had before, except he'd removed the cigarettes. His old friend had been on his ass about giving up smoking, and had now done his little part to make sure it would happen.

Falau reached first into the glove, box and then the center console, and again find nothing. He shook his head and banged his fist on the steering wheel in frustration. There was no way he could stop at a convenience store to get cigarettes at a time like this. Suddenly, looking back into his rearview mirror again he saw an oncoming black Humvee racing up behind him. The car looked more like something out of the military than the kind you would find at your local dealer.

The car was bearing down on him hard, and he had the sinking feeling the guards were back on to him.

Falau pulled over to the side of the road to allow the Humvee to go by, but instead it came up hard and pulled in front of him at an angle to box him in. The back door opened to reveal a man with a handgun drawn. He wore sunglasses and the same suit as the rest of John Wise's guards. He lifted the gun and took aim at Falau, and fired one shot that ricocheted off the bulletproof windshield.

Falau dropped the van into reverse and pushed his foot down on the gas as hard as possible, causing the tires to spin and squeal as the van lurched backward. Shoving his foot hard on the brake and pushing the transmission into drive, the car locked up and spun around, shooting him forward.

The Humvee was quick and nimble for its size, and much like the van Falau drove, was not straight out of a showroom. It had been modified, improved, and made into an attack machine.

The Humvee raced up tight to the bumper of the Caravan and shunted hard against it.

A man in the Humvee waved a shotgun outside the window and took aim at the racing Caravan in front of him. He fired one shot that slammed into the back window of the Dodge, splintering the glass into a massive spider web waiting to fall away.

Falau cut the wheel hard, pulling it to the side and then back the other way. The Humvee stayed in close contact as Falau bit into corners and turned, trying to beat the bigger car with precision rather than flat-out speed.

The Humvee was up to the task, riding close on his bumper with the guard still aiming and ready to take him out.

Falau pushed the gas as hard as it would go and felt the engine straining. The Humvee pulled up next to him, getting itself in position to clip the back quarter of his car to cause a spin out and possibly a rollover.

Falau could see the driver eyeballing his back tire as he looked through the side-view mirror, and quickly stepped on his brakes, pulling back into a side-by-side position with the Humvee. The back window of the Humvee rolled down, and a man wearing the familiar suit hung out the window as the two cars pressed closer and closer together. He reached out, trying to grasp the handle of the sliding door of the Caravan.

Falau swerved out, then in, and out again, trying to strike fear into the man that he could get crushed between the two cars as the race continued. But the man had no such reaction, and he stayed steadfast in his task and eventually grabbed onto the handle and pulled it open, causing the door to slide back.

As he saw the man Falau cut the wheel again, hard to the right, forcing himself into the side of the Humvee. The guard hanging out the side pulled himself away just in time, but as Falau cut back again the other way a hand reached out from the Humvee grabbing onto the frame of the door.

The guard's horrific, blood-curdling scream rang out through the air, causing all heads to turn, including Falau's, who looked back to see blood rolling down the guard's hand as he grabbed tight to the front door frame. The van's doors had been finished with razor blade sharpness that Tyler had forgotten to tell him about. It was obviously developed for exactly this kind of situation; an unwanted intruder entering the van without permission. The blade was more obvious now Falau could see it, its edge running from top to bottom and across the top beam as well.

Keeping pace, the Humvee tried to pull closer, seeing that the man could not pull his hand away. The blade dug deep into the flesh and the man yanked with all his might, but the blade had sunk deep and hard into the bone.

Feeling his animalistic side rear its ugly head again, Falau knew he could simply hit hard into the Humvee and dislodge the man. But that wouldn't take care of the situation. Falau looked at the console on the car and flipped a switch that he knew would close the side door. The door slowly crept forward, closing inch by inch. The guard was still unable to remove his doomed hand.

The young guard yanked harder and harder, despite the pain and the screams.

The door slid ever closer, now within a foot. The man leaned out the window even further as Falau started to drift away from the Humvee.

"NO!" screamed the guard as the door crushed down on his hand. The sliding door showed no mercy, and simply kept closing until it reached its final destinations, with the strength of the *jaws of life*, the device used to pry open cars with trapped people inside. Falau heard the blade cutting through the bone, severing the man's hand in half as the door finally slammed into its locking position.

Falau looked back and saw the man's hand and fingers sticking inside the car, and he yanked the wheel hard to the left in a final attempt to completely sever the hand from the man's arm. The man was yanked from the window of the Humvee and was now being dragged on the outside of the car, his shins and feet dragging on the ground, the underside of the back wheel almost sucking him under and running him over.

Falau looked to the console again and flipped the switch. The door made a clicking sound and crept open. The guard screamed again as he saw the door moving forward, and reached with his other hand to try to grasp onto it, but as the door opened about four inches his severed hand fell inside the van as the rest of his body flopped to the ground, smacking hard off the tarmac as the Caravan's wheels drove right over him, crushing his body and causing blood to splatter from his face and torso.

Falau let the door slide fully open, and glanced into the back and saw the severed hand rolling around as he swerved from side to side, blood smearing the door and the rear floor.

The guards in the Humvee were now ready to fight having just seen their brother fall. Opening fire mercilessly on the Caravan from the passenger side of the Humvee, a man rested his butt on the outside of his window, leaning across the hood of the Humvee and firing an automatic rifle into the side and back of the open door. The window that had just been occupied by the fallen guard was now filled by another man with a shotgun he had leveled at Falau.

Boom! The shotgun exploded, causing pellets to fly everywhere inside the van. Falau felt several pellets stab into his body.

"Moron! Too stupid, even for you!" shouted Falau, realizing that if the man had used the buckshot more commonly used for shooting birds than the hard-round slugs, it would have acted more like bullets.

Falau activated the sequence on the dash that made the back seats roll in and the turret machine guns rise up. He used the radio knob to tune them in and put on their tracking device, then hit the button to fire.

Tap tap tap tap tap tap...

The machine guns rang out with ferocity and power, and ripped a straight line across the side of the Humvee and found their mark on the young man hanging out the window with the shotgun. A mess of red and gray lay on the top of the Humvee and its side window, where the young man's brains had been deposited after the machine gun destroyed his head. The guard on the far side of the car firing the M16 pulled himself back inside.

It was now obvious to Falau that the Humvee was also bulletproofed, so as long as the two stayed inside the car his weapons would be useless for attack.

Seeing a row of telephone poles down the right side of the road Falau, closed into the Humvee.

He quickly set the internal system for the machine guns to fire more rapidly and precisely at the window of the driver side door, opening them up to their maximum.

As the driver steered to the left Falau triggered the machine guns to fire. The Humvee driver was met with a barrage of bullets crashing into the window just inches from his face. He pulled his head down to the right to avoid any breaking glass.

Timing his move for maximum effect, Falau jammed the front of the Dodge Caravan hard into the Humvee, pushing it to the right and straight into one of the telephone poles.

The Humvee wrapped around the pole, causing it to stop instantly and snapping the pole in half. The men inside crashed against the front windshield and collapsed in a heap inside. Falau pushed his foot down on the gas again, soon creating distance between him and the men that would soon come after him.

It was time to regroup and finish this mission.

Chapter 28

SITTING AT THE DESK his fingers floated over the keys on the laptop. His eyes watched the screen as the images appeared, popping up in rapid succession. The feeling deep inside him that he couldn't prevent was going to come on.

Calvin Wise had been spending his days and nights slumped over the keyboard like a writer fixated on his story. But he was flipping from website to website looking for the next woman that would deserve his love. He wanted to get all of her love, and the only way he thought he could was causing her death with his own hands.

The women were not just faces and names. He saw each one is an opportunity to fulfill his deepest desires. He felt them move and look at him as he clicked on each profile. Pausing on one of his favorite sites, he looked at the woman on the screen.

"She's a slut," he muttered to himself looking at the woman and reaching out with his hand to touch her cheek on the screen. "She needs to know what love is. I can fix her. I can show her what true love really is."

The madman shifted from side to side in his chair, anxious to get to the woman he wanted. He pulled the top drawer of his desk open, displaying a number of trinkets that lay in the bottom. An earring, a necklace, a hair tie, and several coins. He scooped them out of the drawer and put them in front of him, admiring them as trophies of his great conquests.

He smiled at the collection, each one a small remembrance from each of the woman that he'd told he 'fully loved.'

"Samantha, you were my favorite," said the killer, picking up a hair band that had held her ponytail in place. "You struggled. Then you gave yourself to me. You just let go. You opened up to true love. You know now what true love is."

"There's more that needs to be done," said the voice in the back of his head. "So many more... so many more."

"I know!"

"You know, but you don't do anything. You're afraid. You can't do this. You're not man enough. You'll never be the man your father is. You'll never be the man you want to be."

"I am a man. I am more of a man than you'll ever know. I've taken life and I've given life, and I'm all that a man can be."

Calvin slammed his hand on the desk, knocking the items to the floor. Then he dropped his head in his hands as he heard a knock on the bedroom door.

"What?"

"Hi. It's Dad. I heard you yelling. Is everything okay?" said a timid voice from the other side of the door.

"I'm fine. Just leave me alone."

"You sounded pretty upset. Is there anything I can do for you?"

"I said fucking leave me alone!"

The door slid open revealing the cautious face of the young killer's father. Not getting too close to the opening, he peered in to see his son sitting in front of the open laptop.

"No need to swear. I was just seeing if you're okay."

"You just won't listen. I try to tell you to go away and you keep coming back."

Pushing the door all the way open John Calvin took a small step forward and stood tall and proud, staring down at his son at the desk.

"We've been down this road before. You don't speak to me that way. I pay the bills. I do all the work. You're just living off me. Once you have your own place and pay your own way, you can tell me what to do there."

Spinning in his chair, disgusted, he turned his back to his father. Calvin crossed his arms like a defiant child.

"What are you doing on the laptop?" he asked, looking across the desk to see what was on the screen. "What the hell is this?"

Calvin reached back with his hands and slammed the top of the laptop shut. "None of your business."

"The hell it isn't."

"What do you want from me?"

"Another girl has gone missing! Your computer has that same site up on it. Where are you going at night?"

"I don't care if some whore got killed. She probably deserved it."

"The police have been coming around again. A friend of mine said you were seen in the area of one of the killings. What the hell is wrong with you?"

"He doesn't respect you," whispered the voice living in Calvin's head. "He knows you're weak. He has never respected you."

"No!" squealed Calvin, pounding his fist on the desk and causing all his trophies to scatter.

Calvin's father looked down at the desk and spotted Calvin's trophies, now strewn all over the place. He grabbed a hair ribbon and held it up. "Who's this from?"

"Nobody."

"Who is it from?" he demanded, insisting on an answer.

"I said nobody!"

"Is this from a girl you've hurt?" he asked, his voice quivering and sounding somewhere between tears and rage. "Did you hurt her? Who is she?"

Reaching out, Calvin ripped the ribbon from his father's thick, strong hands. "That belongs to me. I earned it. Me!"

"You earned nothing! If it wasn't for me you would be rotting your life away in prison right now."

"Look how he treats you," whispered the voice. "He has no idea what you can do. He will never respect you until you prove you're a man."

Calvin stood up from his chair and turned to his father, his face hardened. His eyes had lost all life. He pushed the chair under the desk and took two steps toward his father, pausing inches from his face.

John Wise lost all authority, as his eyes questioned what his son was doing and what he may do to him. His mouth gaped, as if he were searching for something to say. The child he had known and the young man he had called his son had just vanished before his eyes, replaced by a monster who had possessed the vessel that was his son.

"Father, you should watch your tone with me. You have no idea who I am or what I can do. I might as well be a stranger to you, and you know what they say..." He inched closer and locked eyes with the older man. "Don't talk to strangers!"

Chapter 29

HIS SHAKING HANDS MADE it damn near impossible to get the key into the lock. Placing one hand over the other Falau guided the key, only catching the top opening to the keyhole, his efforts were more reminiscent of a man using a sledgehammer than a surgeon.

Finally, the door swung open, the knob on the inside leaving a dent on the wall from the impact. Falau moved quickly, closing the door and locking it, both the chain and the deadbolt. He moved to the window and looked out, being sure to keep himself to the side so he could not be seen. He saw a few hookers on the corner and the same old daytime traffic. Nothing out of the ordinary.

On the coffee table were the new 9mm bullets for Falau's gun, and he loaded two magazines as fast as he could before tucking them into his back pockets. The remaining ten bullets he put in his front pockets.

"It will be just my luck to get shot there and blow off my own dick," Falau said to himself while putting on a new shirt.

Knock, Knock.

Freezing in place Falau glanced at the door. He could see in the gap beneath it there were two sets of feet standing right outside the door, their shadows giving away their number.

Working on light feet the big man moved to the side-wall, staying out of sight in case the men in the hall looked through the peep-hole. Gently reaching down with his eyes on the door he picked up his Ruger SR9C and slid it into the back of his pants.

Eyes fixed on the door and stood in position for a forced entry, the doorknob jiggled. He watched the slightest movement, but then the men on the far side of the door shook it with more force and pulled hard against the handle.

KNOCK! KNOCK! KNOCK!

"We know you're in there, Falau, so open the door!" shouted a man whose voice Falau had no recollection of.

"Who is it?" replied Falau in a high-pitched female voice, mocking the men outside. He rummaged through the papers on the coffee table looking for the card with Tyler's phone number.

A loud clunk against the door caused the frame to crack. And then again, as the man outside the door kicked with all of his might, smashing the door from its frame. No matter how good the locks were, this man was going to drive his way through.

The frame finally gave way and the door fell into the apartment. Falau slid himself down between the bed and the sofa, using the sofa for cover, but nobody entered the room. Falau looked around the room for possible escape routes in case something was thrown in. The window was the only possibility, and that would be a nasty fall, making it near impossible to get up and get safely away after.

"Falau, we're not here for trouble. We just need to talk with you. We're going to walk in. No need to get jumpy about anything."

"You always kick down the doors of people you just want to talk with?"

A chuckle floated from the hallway. "I understand your trepidation. We're going to come in. We just want to talk."

Two large men dressed in the all too familiar suits entered the room, and looked like carbon copies of one another. Both in their forties, short haircuts, fit, and not a thread out of place... the kind of men who did everything by the book and had total loyalty to their boss. They were mercenaries.

The odds that these two were here and that nobody else knew were slim. They were just the first wave, and more guards were sure to come.

Edging away from his partner one of the guards went to the far side of the room, setting up a tactical advantage. Falau mapped their distance, knowing he had already been seen but not wanting to show himself for fear they could fall into attack mode.

"Mr. Falau, this is quite a place you have here," said the guard closest to the door as he slid his hand across the top of the sofa and inspected the grime on his hand.

"Well, my summer place is in the Hamptons," quipped Falau, raising his body inch by inch and revealing his position to the two men.

"Sir, there's no need to be shy. We just want to talk."

"Say what you need to say, then leave."

"Why so hostile?"

"Well, you just cost me my security deposit on the apartment by breaking down the door."

"You like to joke, don't you, Mr. Falau?" asked the guard at the far side of the room as he unbuttoned his sports jacket. "You're quite the character. You keep showing up at Mr. Wise's house. You got out of jail somehow. All very impressive. The problem is that we can't have you coming around."

"I was just looking to take a few pictures."

The guard across the room nodded. "Mr. Falau, do you think we're fools?"

"I don't know you that well, but I'm sure you do your best."

The guard smiled. "We can't have you poking around the property. You need to come with us. We can do it the easy way or the hard way, but no matter what you leave with us.

Falau's senses jumped to high alert, his mind taking in all the information of the room and the two men. He knew deep down where the men were headed. The bulge in their jackets showed they had handguns in chest holsters that could be drawn and fired in less than two seconds.

"Sorry, but I have dinner reservations with an old friend. Need to take a rain check with you boys." Falau shifted his footing, bringing his left foot forward and squaring himself up to both men the best he could, his eyes focused on their distance to each other and from him.

The guard on the far side of the room would have a straight shot. He was in line with Falau. The guard at the door would need to reach away from Falau on the opposite side of his body, then pull the gun back across, taking a second longer.

"You're going to break your plans tonight," said the furthest guard while taking a step toward Falau. "In fact, I don't think you're ever going to have dinner again."

Drifting his hand slowly behind his back the big man knew that his every move was being watched. Nothing would come as a surprise. Moving at a lackluster pace, he pulled the 9mm from the back of his pants and brought it down by his side in full view.

"What have you got there? A cap gun?" joked the guard across the room.

"I think he has his sister's gun," quipped the nearest guard.

"It's a 9mm. It can do the job."

"Oh. Can it? You just brought a fly swatter to a gunfight, boy," said the far guard, pulling open the side of his sports jacket to expose his firearm that held far more power than the 9mm. "Smith & Wesson, 357 Magnum. Something for a man."

"Wow. Impressive gun. But not for me. I'm not really into ballistic masturbation."

The guard grimaced, tired of playing. "Time to go."

"I don't think so."

"Let's get him."

The two guards took a step toward Falau, their hands moving inside their sports jackets to reach for their handguns.

Falau squeezed the handgrip of the Ruger as his eyes narrowed, his finger dropping from the side of the barrel onto the trigger.

Did I put a bullet in the chamber? he thought, feeling the world fall into slow motion around him.

The guards had now secured their guns and were both within five-feet of him.

Falau lifted the gun, shooting from the hip at the guard to the right. The bullet hit him center mass, just as he'd been taught years ago. Hit your target in their biggest spot. Right in the chest.

The bullet exploded just as Tyler had shown Falau it would in the lab. The Kevlar vest under the guard's shirt was ripped to pieces as the explosion ruined the man's chest.

By instinct, the other guard immediately snapped his head around to assess the situation, rather than keeping his eyes on his target.

Falau shifted his hips and dropped to one knee, limiting the need to shoot across his body. Firing off a single round, the bullet again found its target in the center of the guard's chest, the explosion having the same devastating effect.

Both men dropped to the floor in a pool of their own blood. Dead.

Falau stared at the men, unsure what to do next.

Chapter 30

B lood started seeping away from the dead bodies lying on the floor. Falau shook his head, trying to bring himself back into the present.

Rushing to the fallen door he lifted it with ease, pushing it back into place before the nosy neighbors could come and inspect what was going on. *The police must have been called*, thought Falau as he frantically moved about the apartment searching for something–anything–that could help.

"Focus!" Falau demanded of himself. "Slow down and focus. The bodies first."

Racing to the bathroom Falau ripped down the shower curtain and rushed back into the living room. Laying it on the floor he examined if both bodies would fit inside it.

"Bleach!" he said aloud, running into the kitchen and pulling open the cabinet doors under the sink. Yanking aside the various bottles of cleaners and solvents he could see there was no bleach.

Back in the living room he caught his breath, and put his foot on the coffee table. But he suddenly pulled his leg back, causing him to tumble to the floor in a heap in the pool of blood, and finding himself looking eye-to-eye with a dead man. The man's eyes had already started to cloud over so they looked fake, like a doll's eyes. Yet there was nothing to indicate the man was just verbally sparring with another man just moments before.

Falau pushed himself back, scrambling to get away from the body.

"You killed him. You killed me," whispered the female voice in the back of his head. "His eyes look like mine."

Forcing himself to his feet, Falau grabbed the half-finished bottle of whiskey that had sat next to his bed for months. He opened the top and took a long slug, swallowing several times before stopping.

I'm screwed! he thought.

Knock. Knock. Knock.

Falau again pulled the gun from the back of his pants and pointed it at the door.

A voice called through the door. "Mr. Falau. We've been sent by Tyler to help with your problem. May we come in?"

The name Tyler raced through Falau's head, stopping all confusion. Tyler was an anchor. Something to depend upon. If the people on the other side of the door knew Tyler, then they were on his side.

"Come in," he said, wondering if he were making a mistake that could end his life in a matter of moments.

"Thank you, Sir."

The door opened and five men entered the room, closing the door behind them.

A young man no older than Falau himself stepped forward. "Mr. Falau, if it's okay I would like to hand out assignments before I speak with you."

Falau nodded, impressed with the man's confidence and ability not to be phased by two dead men on the floor.

"You two are on the bodies. You're on floor cleanup. Johnny, you're going to fix the door. We're out of here in five mins max. Let's go."

The men sprang into action so fast that it looked like a blur to Falau. They all worked in silence and perfect unison, like an expert ballet troop that has every move of their show choreographed to perfection, a kind of art, despite the grim nature of the show.

"Mr. Falau, I have a new set of clothing for you, all made to Tyler's specifications. If you could just take off the clothing you have on now and place it in this bag, then put on the new clothes."

Changing his clothes as fast as he could Falau looked out the window after hearing the faint sound of a siren he was sure was coming his way. The bodies had been cleared and the floor was being cleaned. The man on the door had wedged it back in and was hammering in a few nails to keep it from falling back out.

"Where's Tyler?"

"One minute left. Let's go, team," said the young man in a matter-of-fact voice. "I'm sorry, Sir, but Tyler is not here. He sent us in to take care of this issue. It's what we do. I think we all knew that something like this was a possibility considering the case you're working on."

"Why not just give me some guards?" asked Falau while pulling on the new pants.

"That could blow your cover, Sir. Please, we need to leave," the young man said with all the calmness of a preacher talking to an old lady. "Time's up, men. Out, now."

The men on the bodies were already long gone. The cleaner and the man fixing the door hustled out the door, closely followed by Falau and the young man.

Hitting the street they all went to separate cars and drove away.

"Mr. Falau, the van is set for you. Here are the keys. Please don't leave them in the ignition again. Good luck," he said, starting to walk away.

"Wait!" said Falau. "What do I do now?"

"Complete your mission, of course."

Chapter 31

His backside hit the driver's seat as he heard the police sirens cars getting closer. The key was in the ignition, avoiding the problems he had earlier with the apartment door. A quick turn, and the engine came to life. Grabbing the gear shift on the steering column, he dropped it into drive and pulled away in a casual and methodical manner.

Police cars raced up Massachusetts Avenue, hitting the intersection of Columbus Avenue just as the light turned green and Falau was driving by them in the opposite direction, keeping his head fixed forward and making no eye contact with the police in the cars flying past him.

He kept going straight through the intersection and drove up to the next, taking a right on Huntington Avenue toward the Prudential Center. Falau was sure that the mix and twist of roads would expose anyone who may be following him, though the idea that more guards were on the way had not escaped his mind. Perhaps they were just waiting outside for him to leave and then start the chase again.

"Hello," said a voice behind him.

"Oh!" The word shot from his mouth as he jumped in his seat, his heart rate doubled. Instinctively his hand reached back for the 9mm tucked into the back of his jeans.

The sounds of the voice filtered in his mind and was rapidly deciphered, as the next words came forth from the back seat.

"Sorry. Didn't mean to frighten you," said Tyler in a calm and soothing tone. "Don't shoot me."

"Shit! What the hell did you do that for?" questioned Falau, knowing full well why Tyler needed to be secretive with everything he did.

"There were a lot of eyes back there so I just laid under a blanket back here until you got going. Out of sight, out of mind."

Falau looked in the rearview mirror and saw his friend sitting in the back seat of the van. His hair and suit looked impeccable, despite his claim he'd been under a blanket waiting for the right time to pop up.

"Thanks for the cleanup crew. I figured I was screwed with them kicking down the door and me shooting them."

"No problem. After you got out this morning I was thinking Wise might have gotten word of it. A man like that would rather just kill you at this point than stick you back in jail."

"Nice to know."

Sitting in silence the two men sized one another up. Falau wondered why Tyler was in his car now.

Tyler looked side to side out the windows, fidgeting in his seat. He looked like a preacher who had forgotten his sermon and was looking for the right thing to say.

"Falau, I have always been straight with you and there is no need to change that now. Is this all too much for you?"

"What?"

"Is this all too much for you?"

"You're kidding me, right?" Falau's tone switched to anger as his fist pounded on the steering wheel. "In the last eight hours I have escaped from jail. I've been in a car chase where I probably killed four people.

I killed two more people in my apartment at point blank range, and you're asking me if I'm up for this. My whole fucking life is into this!"

Tyler straightened his coat and looked down at the ground, giving Falau a few moments to compose himself and take the steam out of a potential argument.

"We go back a long way. I care about you and what happens to you. I know your history. Even the stuff you won't talk about. Like your empathy."

Falau's strong, calloused hands gripped the steering wheel hard, and he pulled it toward himself trying to exert some of the negative energy building up inside him.

"My history has nothing to do with this mission. I can do my job and I'm getting sick of you asking me if I want out. If I want out, I will tell you. Until then you don't need to ask me."

"That's part of my job. I need to make sure you're okay. You've given a lot to this mission, including going to prison. If you said screw this, it would be understood. We don't expect anyone to be superhuman. The last thing anyone wants is to see this thing tear you apart. There is no shame in walking away. You have to come first."

Falau could not bring himself to look in the rearview mirror. He knew Tyler was right, but he was angry about Tyler changing his tune just hours after saying there was too much to do, and that Falau could not take a few days for himself. Was Tyler screwing with him and seeing what he could take? Was this all a test from the judges?

"Thank you for your concern about me," said Falau with a dusting of sarcasm in his voice. "This is all I have. I have no woman, no job, and no life. I struggle to get by every day. This is what I want, and this is what I need. Besides, I need to take care of this for T-Bone. I made him a promise."

"You convicts all stick together," said Tyler, trying to hold back his laughter

Falau smiled and nodded his head, looking back in the mirror.

"I know you're just concerned about me, but you just have to let me go and do the job. You can't be worried about me. Let me do my thing and you will not be disappointed. I promise you that."

"I know. I can trust you, but as a friend I just needed to check in. Killing six people in one day is not something anyone can just shake off. You're my man on this job and any others that come up in the future. Just don't let it get too personal. Personal feelings just cloud a person's judgment."

"I understand," said Falau. The big man felt a weight lift off his chest, the way it always did when he and Tyler finished fighting. The two men had always fought and defended each other like brothers, and now was no different.

"Pull over here," said Tyler as they pulled up to a stop-light.

"I can drive you where you need to go."

"No need. This will be fine."

Falau pulled the car to the side of the road and hit the button for the side door to open. Tyler jumped out and pulled his jacket tight around him as the sun started to set.

"Good luck. Call me if you need me."

"Will do."

Chapter 32

STANDING MOTIONLESS outside his son's bedroom, Calvin Wise's father held up a fist ready to knock at the door. But something held him back. Feeling a lump rise in his throat, he felt as if he was going to cry. Each interaction with his son was getting more and more strange. The young man, who was once such an inquisitive and dynamic person, had now become a shell of his former self.

Inside the door a voice could be heard but not made out. It was one side of a conversation, but nobody was in the room other than Calvin. If there had been someone there, the guards would have let him know.

Holding his breath he pulled his hand back, fearing what it could lead to. What state was Calvin in now? Was he calm? Was he angry? It was impossible to tell.

Knock. Knock. Knock.

Silence hung in the air.

Knock. Knock. Knock.

Again, nothing.

"Calvin? Everything okay?" asked his father, turning the knob and opening the door. "How's it going buddy?"

Calvin sat motionless with his back to the door and facing away from his father. He stared straight ahead.

Looking down at the desk the older man saw a collage of pictures with small objects on each of them. It looked like a work in progress. "You working on something?"

Calvin held silent and motionless.

Mr. Wise looked closer at the pictures on the desk and recognized the faces from the evening news. The girls who had gone missing were all there, each of them with a small trinket attached to the picture. They were the same things that Calvin refused to let him see earlier. The girl's eyes looked up at him, their names printed with care across the bottom of each picture.

Sandy Withcom

Jennifer Lathum

Alexa Sonberg

Mary Kellen

Erica Jones

Samantha Erickson

His mouth dropped open as his mind filled with a thick fog trying to make sense of what he was seeing. *How could this be real? Why?*

The chair creaked as Calvin turned to face his father. His face was drawn and empty, like people in shock after a great trauma. His voice was void of emotion and he made no eye contact with his father. "Why are you in my room?"

"Calvin, what is all this? Did you hurt these girls? Don't you know the trouble you could get in for even having these pictures?"

"This is none of your business."

"The guards tell me you go out each night, and now I see these girls on your desk. The same ones who have been killed! Did you hurt them?" asked Mr. wise, raising his voice as frustration grew inside him. "You're going to get caught. Is that what you want? A life in prison! What's happened to you?"

Tilting his head upward the young man finally made eye contact with his father.

"He doesn't respect you," whispered the voice in his mind, yet sounding far away.

Placing his hands on the arms of the chair Calvin pushed hard upwards, shooting him to his feet and launching the chair backward, crashing it into the wall.

Taking a step toward his father he locked eyes with the man.

With a hard gaze that felt as if it was digging into his soul, John Wise felt frozen in place, unable to react to the monster that his son had become.

"You have no idea how hard things are for me. I have never been good enough for you and your high standards. Not good enough at school, my grades, jobs, girlfriend! Nothing!"

"Where is this coming from?"

"He thinks you're a fool. He expects you to believe he doesn't understand. He thinks you're stupid," whispered the voice, closer this time.

"I've always been pushed aside for my brother and sister. You always said they were older so they could go first, but the truth is you loved them more. I was always in last place with you. They were your little confidants, while I had the nerve to be outspoken. So I paid the price when mom died, left alone with all of you. Nobody on my side!"

The space between them had disintegrated to less than six inches, as each of the men stared into one another's eyes trying to make sense of the situation and their relationship.

"You never had time for me!" Calvin said, turning away to the desk. The young man lifted his hands out to the side like a preacher, passing them over the twisted collage he had created on the desk. "But this was just for me. These girls belong to me. I showed them true love. I showed them how to give themselves fully to me. I saved them from the slut-whore lives they lived."

Calvin's eyes shone as the tears started to fall down his cheeks. "If you had just loved me, if you had just accepted whatever I did and told me it was great the way other parents do, then I wouldn't have needed to help these girls. I just wanted your approval."

Turning back to his father Calvin wiped the tears from his eyes with the back of his hand. He gasped for air as another wave of weeping overcame him.

"Did I do good with the girl's, Dad?" Calvin asked, picking up the pictures on the desk and trying to place them into his father's unaccepting hands. "I am the best at saving them, right? Say I'm the best at saving them."

His father's mouth moved slightly, but with no words uttered. Standing in silence the older man looked at his son, wondering what he was trying to tell him. *He killed the girls, right?* he thought. *He killed them all. For me. Why? No.*

The pictures fell from Calvin's hands, decorating the floor in a macabre tableau. The tears fell hard from his eyes and he reached out to his father, stepping closer to him and looking for a hug. "Dad. Are you proud of me?"

As Calvin's hands reached his father's shoulders Mr. Wise raised his own hands against Calvin's chest, stopping him from getting closer.

Calvin's body locked up and his tears immediately stopped.

"You're insane, Calvin. We need to get you help," said Mr. Wise in a voice that lacked empathy. "You're a serial killer. This was no mistake. You meant to kill those girls. How... how could you do that?"

"I did it for you. You can't reject me now. This is perfection. Nobody could do it better than I did."

Pulling back, Mr. Wise's eyes filled with tears. "You can't be my son. My son would never do something like this. You're no son of mine."

"He hates you. He thinks you're weak. You need to help him see the light," whispered the voice.

"What?" asked Calvin, stepping closer to his father. "Even this is not good enough for you? What could I have done better?"

Taking a step back and trying to keep a distance from Calvin, John Wise kept his eyes locked on his son who was steadily closing in.

"You don't have an answer, do you? Not a fucking thing could I have done better! But to you this is just another thing I have screwed up."

"Keep back, Calvin," said his father, lifting a hand.

"You hate me. I will always be a loser to you, even when I give you a gift as good as this. You need me to help you!" shouted the young man, taking another step closer.

"You need help. We can get you help. Now step back!" insisted his father, fumbling to find the door with his hand.

"Oh no, you're going to put me away, to stop me from talking about what you do. No, not me, you're not going to do that to me. You have sinned! You forgot how to love fully!"

The door jamb struck hard against Mr. Wise's shoulder as he turned to run. Fingers scratched down the back of his neck as he was pulled back by his shirt collar and dragged to the ground. Calvin's fist rose high into the air, striking down hard on his father's ear as the fist hit its target. He slumped to the side trying to pull together his thoughts.

Cavin's feet walked by, closing the door to the bedroom. Turning back the young man kicked hard into his father's face, obliterating his nose and causing a wild stream of blood to pour down his face.

Kicking hard again, Calvin's foot connected with his father's midsection, causing him to roll over onto his back.

"Did I kick you well enough, father, or will I miss dessert because I messed that up too?" mocked the crazed young man.

Reaching down and grabbing his father's shirt Calvin dragged him to the bed and threw him on it.

"I will never let you doubt me again."

"Save him. Like you saved the girls," whispered the voice.

"I need to show you how good I am. It's the only way you'll respect me. It's the only way I can save you."

Climbing on the bed and straddling his father Calvin looked down into his eyes.

"Calvin... No," gasped his father, his eyes pleading for forgiveness and mercy.

Sighing deeply, Calvin smiled at his father. "I love you Dad."

A smile crossed Mr. Wise's face and his eyes closed on hearing the first tender thing his son had said in a long time.

Calvin's hands suddenly slid over his father's chest and wrapped around his neck.

His father's eyes opened, realizing Calvin had no intention of stopping and that his 'I love you' was more of a goodbye.

The killer dropped his head onto his father's chest and pushed out his elbows to fend off any blows, like he had done every time before.

He tightened his grip as his father tried to punch him. He could feel the pulse of his carotid artery getting stronger as it constricted, the blood trying to force its way through the smaller opening.

"This is how I killed the girls. I like making it last. I like feeling their deaths. I'm saving you from yourself. I wonder what prize I will find in your pocket for me to keep."

Fighting to speak, the killer's father begged. "No... No!"

"I'll show you that I can finish the job. Just like you always told me to do."

His hands tightened further around the neck of his victim, causing the man to thrash uncontrollably while desperately searching for air. His blows no longer had any power and he felt himself slipping away into the darkness.

"This is my favorite part, Dad. The part where I feel the life leave your body. It's magical."

Calvin gave one more long, hard squeeze, accompanied by a primordial moan, until his father moved no more.

Releasing his fingers, Calvin lifted his head and checked for a pulse.

Nothing.

A smile filled the young man's face as he looked down at his dead father.

"You're welcome, Dad."

Chapter 33

THE SCARRED AND BATTERED Dodge Caravan pulled up the street with its lights off, Falau parking in the same spot it had the last two times he had visited the Wise home. Falau killed the engine then cranked the driver's side window down.

The air was still with a clear sky overhead, yet despite being in the suburbs the stars were barely visible due to all the light pollution emanating from Boston just a few miles away.

Rubbing his growing beard, Falau kept his eyes on the front gate. Drawing the guards out would give him an idea whether or not they were still at full protection in the house, but if they did not come out it was probable that his dismantling of the men in the Humvee and the guards that came to his apartment had left them in a weakened state. That could be the opening he was looking for.

Lifting the binoculars to his face he scanned over the yard and saw nothing had changed. The dogs were still out and patrolling in a pack. The floodlights outside the home were on timers and turned on and off every ten minutes. Cameras sat in trees in the corners of the yard, and kept an eye on anyone who dared cross the grass. Four cars sat in the driveway, two of which were older and utilitarian looking and probably owned by the guards still inside. They were nothing like the vehicles the Wise family would drive.

Pulling a pack of cigarettes from his pocket he tapped them against his hand and pulled one from the box. Cupping his hands in front of it, he lit the match and took a long breath in, holding the smoke deep inside before letting it out in a long slow stream.

"Friggin' Dogs," he said to himself, watching the pack of Rottweilers chase a squirrel into a tree, barking loud and aggressively around the trunk. A few even tried to jump and scale the tree before falling back to the ground. They didn't just want to chase the square... they wanted to kill it. The way they appeared, Falau thought they were willing to kill anything they could get their teeth into. *No cover at all. Just run for the door. It's the only way.*

The lights in the house started turning off one by one in a specific pattern, as if someone was walking room to room and switching them off manually. Homes of this class may have bedrooms with free control of the lights, but most of the other rooms were kept on timers and ran through a central security system. This would make sure that if anyone did think about robbing the home they would never be sure if people were awake inside. Besides, the guards would still need to make their regular rounds around the property, and hallway lights would most definitely stay on for that.

Looking down at his cell phone he pressed the button on the side to illuminate the screen. 10:38pm. Looking back up at the house and then back to the phone, he knew that nobody would ever set timers for such a random time, especially not rolling from one room to another. This was intentional and being carried out by someone inside the house. *But why?* he wondered, lifting the binoculars and seeing if he could catch a glimpse of somebody walking by a window.

Needing a closer look he opened the door and stepped out. He surveyed the area around him, and still saw no guards. He knew he was in plain sight of their equipment, but were they just choosing to leave him alone? Unlikely. He'd been far too much of a pain in their necks to just let him camp out in front of the house.

Reaching back, he made sure that the Ruger SR9C sat in its normal place, tucked into his jeans against his lower back. The gun had already saved his life from the two guards, and there was no way he would enter the home without it.

He walked briskly across the street to the wall that surrounded the Wise home. Staying tight against it he walked on, trying to see if he could draw out the guards. His stride was methodical and leisurely, like an older man seeking to get in his nightly exercise before bed. Eyes fixated on the gate, he waited for someone to come out. But still nothing happened.

He drew closer to the gate and finally he stood right in front of it. Still nothing. Looking up the driveway as he passed by, he saw nobody. The small guard shack next to the gate was empty. If someone were to pull up to the house now there was nobody there to let them in.

"What the hell?" Falau whispered to himself as he cleared the gate and continued on.

This isn't what a man in Wise's position does. He's totally vulnerable. Something is wrong in that house, thought Falau, returning to the gate. Opportunity had shown itself to the big man, and he was more than ready to take it.

Back at the gate he planted one foot hard against the wall and the other onto the fence. Scaling the gate proved to be easy, with its ornamental wrought iron frame providing grips and footholds easily able to support him. As he reached the top he rolled his body over and dropped to the other side, landing in a military stance. Sprinting up the driveway he scanned the scene for the dogs. If they attacked he could only hope one of the cars was unlocked and he could duck inside. But now all he could hope to do was close the gap.

SITTING IN A HARD WOODEN chair Calvin Wise stared into a computer screen with a blank expression on his face. Next to him on the floor lay the bodies of two guards that worked in his home, their blood spilled across the floor from the wounds where a knife had been ripped across their necks in a savage display of murder.

"Another friend is coming to see us," he said aloud to the dead bodies on the floor.

On the computer screen a young man rushed up the driveway looking around in all directions while keeping himself low. He appeared to know what he was doing.

"I know you. You're the one who keeps coming to take my picture. This will be nice... I can answer all your questions and show you all the good work I've done."

Chapter 34

MAKING IT SAFELY TO the cars the Falau ducked down behind the four-door Mercedes parked closest to the house. The garage door was closed and there was no point just walking up to the front door and ringing the bell.

He spied an opening between the bushes and the side of the garage that rolled downhill to the back of the house, and scurried over to it. The closest wall was still more than a hundred yards away, so if the Rottweilers made their way to him he had no way to escape. At the bottom of the hill where the house turned to the back, he peered around the corner and saw a servant's entrance he was unable to see from the road. It was nestled between two hills and had a small road that led out to a gate on the far side of the property by the lake.

A van was backed up to the door. It was all white, with Permoski's Fine Meats written on the side.

Falau kept close to the ground and crept up to the side window and looked inside, but there was no activity. He placed his hand on the hood of the car and felt the cool metal against his hand, and knew at once the van had been sitting there for quite some time. If it had been driven recently then the hood would have still been warm.

Adjusting himself to look through the back window he saw no activity inside the house where the van was parked. The lights were all off. The van must have been left by the butler, due to his job not being finished.

Reaching into his coat pocket Falau pulled out a pair of black leather gloves, that fit his hands perfectly and eliminated the worry of fingerprints being left around the house. They afforded him the opportunity to look through the building and touch things without having to waste time wiping them down after.

Turning the knob to the back door, it clicked and opened. Suddenly, the sound of aggressive barking from the side of the house started to build, and Falau turned to see the Rottweilers staring at him from the far corner. They broke into a charge in unison, and looked far larger from this close up, maybe a hundred-and-ten-pounds each. Their teeth were exposed and their jowls flapping as they ran, it was pure muscle in motion, like a great sprinter or speed skater.

Falau slid in the door and shut it as fast and quietly as he could. The dogs banged against the door and jumped up at the window, barking and scrapping with one another. Falau dropped low and pulled himself next to a table in case someone came to investigate the noise.

After a few minutes of silence, he heard the dogs break off into another run, their attention diverted elsewhere by some blowing leaves or a skunk.

Standing, he moved gently to the side of the room, assessing everything he saw in front of him. The room was the size of a restaurant kitchen and set up much the same. A line for cooking sat along the wall, with stoves, microwaves, skillets, deep fryers and a grilling station. Further away a pastry section was set up around refrigerators and a walk-in freezer. Directly in front of him was a meat preparation section, most likely where the man from Permoski's Fine Meats did his job. A man of Mr. Wise's wealth could afford to have the butcher come to his home each day and cut select meats for his meals, all at a premium of course.

On the wall was an old fashion dumbwaiter with an electronic key-board. Falau moved in closer to inspect it. He could see there were four floors to the house, including the one he was on. An intercom was embedded into the wall next to the dumbwaiter, assuring that the meal would never sit too long and falling below proper temperature.

The table of the meat carving section held various tools in an oversized butcher's block. Falau ran his hand over it, taking out the cleaver. Spinning it in his hand he could feel the balance was off, its weight drifting to the head too much. He placed it back in the block and pulled out a six-inch flaying knife, quickly placing that back into the block too. Letting his hands wrap wound the series of knives he eventually pulled out a long thick butcher's knife. He swung it in his hand and flipped the blade into the air, grabbing the handle before it hit the metal table. It was perfect. If he did end up in a fight the knife would not give away his position the way a gun would.

The steps from the upper levels dropped down directly behind him without walls to conceal them, so Falau was sure nobody was there. He ascended them as slow and silently as possible, holding the knife to his side. The door at the top was ajar and no lights were on in what Falau assumed was the home's show kitchen. He made out the tile floor; nothing that would be homey enough for a dining room.

He crouched down, opening the door just enough to slip through into the kitchen. He waited, expecting a guard to come charging at him. He'd been exposed far too long on the outside of the house and he was sure there were also cameras inside the house too. But still nothing came.

Falau stood up and saw a hallway just to his side. Pressing his cheek against the corner of the doorway, he looked down exposing as little of himself as possible. He only saw the front door, large and ornate, a double-door that stood ten-feet tall and led into a great foyer with a double staircase like in an old-fashioned movie.

Keeping to the wall the big man slid along toward the front door, all the while keeping his eyes back where he had come from. The foyer was adorned with a large chandelier that hung above the point where the two staircases met. Falau half expected a princess to come walking down at any moment.

The faint sound of music drifted down the steps. It was definite, but too far away to make out the words or the song. Someone was definitely home.

Brandishing the knife in front of him, Falau reached the top of the steps and heard the music getting louder. Death metal, the coarse and ripping guitars and pounding tempo now evident. The singer sang indistinguishable words with his mouth far too close to the microphone to let anyone know what he wanted to say.

Following the music the big man moved to the right, the volume increasing with every step. Reaching the corner he took a peek around and saw a slightly open door with a sliver of light pouring through the gap. Falau thought the music spilling from the opening seemed out of place in a traditional home like this one.

Inching his way closer Falau felt sweat start to build on his neck and hands. The knife was slipping in his hands, and he used the back of his coat to wipe the sweat from dripping down into his eyes. His chest rose and fell in rapid succession as his heart rate rose as his hand reached out to slide open the door.

The music hit him hard as the door fully opened, preventing him from hearing anything other than the grunts and wails of the singer and the shredding guitar riffs.

Falau's eyes squinted against the harsh light. Disoriented, he narrowed his eyes for a better field of vision.

When he finally focused, the hand holding the knife fell to his side. There was a man lying on the bed with blood coming from his mouth, his body not moving.

Falau immediately recognizes the man as Mr. Wise.

Chapter 35

The screeching sound of metal wheels moving fast along a track overcame the sound of the music, but the horrific sound came to a halt with a crashing din of metal vibrating after a sudden stop. The sound came from behind Falau, who took a moment to register it amid the roar of the death metal.

Turning his head behind him and looking out into the hall he saw a young man vaulting himself out of the dumbwaiter on the opposite side. His feet hit the ground, and he was leaping at his target before he could fully turn around.

Caught off guard, Falau felt the full brunt of Calvin driving into him. The young man rammed his shoulder into Falau's upper rib cage, driving him to the ground. The knife slipped from his hands as his head bounced off the floor.

"Ahhhh!" Calvin screamed, reaching for the knife and picking it up in a flash. Turning back to Falau he swung the knife down and sunk it deep into his right shoulder.

"Noooooo!" screamed Falau, feeling the knife cut far into his bone and muscle. Immediately his shirt stained red, spreading from the wound and rapidly expanding.

"Who are you?" shouted Calvin, projecting his voice over the loud music. His hand tightened around the knife and he turned it back and forth, twisting it and chewing up the muscle and tissue inside.

Falau's eyes rolled into his head from the excruciating pain that shot down his arm and across his chest with every small twist of the blade.

Looking up into the killer's face for the first time Falau saw nothing. No gritted teeth, no savagery. He was stone cold, and more than anything appeared apathetic. Falau felt a shiver at the contradiction between what Calvin's body was doing and what his face was showing. It was as if there were two people inside him.

"Answer me," squawked Calvin, yanking the knife from deep inside Falau's shoulder. Raising his hand again the glint of the knife shone beneath the light projecting in the room. He was about to drive it down again, giving Falau just enough time to roll away from the killer. With a sharply placed kick his boot hit the hand wielding the knife, sending it flying across the room.

With pain searing through him from the wound, Falau pulled himself away from the killer, putting distance between them.

Calvin jumped to his feet and charged the big man, only to be met with the heel of a boot driven with force into his knee and causing it to hyper-extend backward. Trying to put weight on the knee made it collapse, giving Falau the chance to regain his feet.

Falau scanned the room for the knife, not knowing the direction it had flown. Taking a step deeper into the room he got a clear look at the young man's father lying dead on the bed. His face had started turning blue and his lips had taken on a purplish hue.

A fist slammed into Falau's back in the location of his kidney, and he gasped for air, dropping to his knees. A hand reached over his shoulder, gripping him by the knife wound and pulling him back. Falau thrashed to get away but the pain was too intense. His head bounced off the hardwood floor, fuzzing his vision for just a moment.

He shook the cobwebs from his mind and turned himself over onto his knees and then back to the center of the room.

Calvin was advancing with the knife in his hand. It had fallen under the desk with the pictures of all the women whose lives he'd stolen.

He was upon Falau in an instant, lunging at him with his knife only to be met with a clean block by Falau, who used both hands to guide the knife aside. Falau gripped tight to the young man's fingers and bent them back, feeling them breaking one by one as the knife dropped to the floor. Falau kicked it, sending it sliding across the floor.

Calvin's face turned red with anger and frustration. He pulled back and butted his forehead as hard as he could into Falau's nose, breaking it instantly and causing the big man to let go.

Falau's eyes filled with water and a wave of nausea overcame him. Buckling over in pain, another kick landed squarely in his midsection to drive the breath from his lungs.

Senses on high-alert, Falau heard Calvin's feet rushing across the floor towards the knife. Then they stopped and he could hear a chair being slid across the floor. Wiping the tears from his eyes he focused to see the killer picking up the knife and turning to face him.

Falau reached back, pulling the 9mm from its spot on his lower back and aimed it directly at Calvin Wise, who froze.

The two stared at one another as the thumping music blared on, deeply out of place in the room of the so-called all-American boy.

Falau cautiously pulled himself to his feet, not taking his eyes off the target. Center mass was where he was aiming.

A laugh bubbled out of Calvin as he stared down the barrel of the 9mm. He looked to the desk and then back at Falau. Raising the hand with the knife he reached with the other for a remote control that sat

9MM   193

on the corner. Hitting the button the music stopped, leaving an eerie silence to fill the air.

"You don't have the balls to shoot me," said Calvin taking a small step forward. "If you did I would be dead by now. Killers don't hesitate. They just do what they need to do. Who are you?"

Falau stood in silence holding the Ruger tight in his hands. Blood still flowed from his knife wound and needed to be packed before he lost much more of the life-giving fluid.

"Look what I did to my dad. It was fun. I saved him. I have saved a lot of evil people from evil things. I delivered them to God."

He took another step closer, smiling, a dead look in his eyes, and motioning to the sides in response to things that were not there.

"You're going to be saved tonight. I will save you. It will feel good. Trust me."

Looking to the knife in his hands, a giggle erupted from the man with the lifeless eyes. His hand dismissively flipped the knife aside, it coming to rest on the bed next to his father's corpse.

"I don't need that. You're going to come along willingly. I bet you're going to feel good. That moment when your life stops. It will be everything you have ever thought it could be," said Calvin, now sounding more like a preacher than a killer. "I wonder what your last expression will be? Maybe fear, maybe terror? Acceptance? No matter what, I will be there looking into your eyes and sharing the moment with you."

The killer moved forward again cutting the space to five feet. The barrel of the 9mm started to tremble in unison with the big man's fear. If he were to shoot Calvin he would need to do it while looking into his eyes.

It would have to be cold-hearted and calculated. A simple decision to end the man's life. Falau didn't know if he could do it.

"You're afraid. I can see it on your face and your shaking hand. You're no killer."

Falau felt a sense of happiness being told he was no killer. If felt good to have those words enter his head after all the times the flashbacks had told him differently.

Stopping a foot away from Falau, the killer held his hands out to the side, tilting his head back and taking a deep breath. "You won't kill me. You can't kill me. It's not in your nature."

The madman lowered his head and let his hands drop down by his sides. He looked down at the gun in Falau's hands and smiled. "Do you think you could kill me with that little gun? You'd be lucky to pierce my skin with that. What is it, a 9mm? My grandmother used to carry one of those."

A look of defeat washed over Falau's face, much to Calvin's delight. He pointed the barrel of the gun up to the ceiling and brought it close to his face. His eyes inspected it and its small size. Maybe Calvin was right, and this gun would not do the job, despite Tyler's special bullets and the history of the gun itself.

Without hesitation Falau's right hand holding the Ruger SR9C struck out, cracking Calvin across the bridge of the nose with the handle of the gun. Calvin dropped to his knees and reached up to hold his nose, that now dripped blood over his shirt and the floor.

Grabbing the killer by the hair, Falau felt the pain shoot through his wound, but he refused to let go. His right-hand pistol-whipped the man several times, spraying more blood over himself and the room.

Letting go of the hair a few chunks remained in his hand, ripped from the scalp during the beating. Calvin fell to the floor in a hefty lump, unconscious.

Looking down at the bloody mess, Falau held the gun in front of him as it dripped with the blood of Calvin Wise.

"Nine millimeters is more than enough!"

Chapter 36

Reaching down to his plain white tube sock Falau stretched the elastic and dug his hand deep inside, emerging with six thick zip-ties made of hard plastic. Their tensile strength far exceeded anything a man could break through with sheer force, and Calvin Wise was certainly not the kind of man who had any of the skills required to slip them once they were on.

Falau's hands worked quickly over the young man's body, placing a zip-tie around each leg and pulling tight. He added a third in the middle, leaving no room for movement. The same procedure was followed with his hands, which were positioned behind his back.

Yanking hard on the middle zip-tie, a moan rumbled up from the bloody face of the killer.

"What are you going to do to me?" he spat, drops of blood flowing from the corner of his mouth. His face lay flush against the hardwood floor and he struggled to lift it. "Who are you?"

Falau ignored the man and kept moving, still unaware if there were any guards left in the house. The clock was ticking and it was time to move before they went on their rounds of the house.

Gathering the pictures and trinket prizes on the desk, Falau folded them with little care and stuffed them into his pocket. Pulling the desk draws open, he rummaged through them but found nothing more of interest.

The laptop sat on the desk. The evidence inside would be more than enough to help the judges make their decision, but it would be cumbersome while trying to move Calvin out of the house. Leaving it behind seemed more prudent.

"Why are you going through my things? Who the hell are you?" Calvin demanded, pulling himself upright and raising his voice. "Don't you know who I am? I am Calvin Wise. Answer me!"

The killer's shouting was now a risk.

Falau ran to the adjoining bathroom and pulled open the closet and the medicine cabinet, sifting through the contents. Returning to the killer Falau held his fist tight, looking down at the young man.

"I'm going to blame you for the killing," Calvin said. "I came in and found you'd killed my dad and then we fought. Who are they going to believe, me or you? Go ahead, bring me to the cops. I'm fine with that."

Smirking and shaking his head at the killer, Falau took a deep breath. With the speed of a cobra his right leg kicked out in a karate style kick, landing directly on Calvin's nose and causing him to scream out in agony.

Falau raised his fist and, putting his whole body weight into the punch, landed squarely on Calvin's chin and rendering him immediately unconscious. Pain shot through Falau's shoulder, but he was now running on adrenalin and ignored his own injury.

"Thought he would never shut up," mumbled the big man to himself as he opened his left hand to reveal a needle and thread. "Everyone should keep duct tape around. You didn't."

Falau fed the thread through the eye of the needled and tied it off. Rolling Calvin onto his back Falau pushed his lips together with one hand as he poked the needle through the skin behind his lips where it was more durable. Working in a methodical fashion Falau's skill at sewing left much to be desired. The thread veered left and right, horribly uneven, but finally he pulled the thread tight, and smirked as Calvin's lips pursed closed as if he was waiting for a kiss.

Dragging the killer into the hallway Falau stuffed his limp body into the dumbwaiter and programed it for the first floor where the cooking area was.

He ran down the steps, foregoing any thought of keeping himself covered. It was now time to go all out and make a break for the fence with his target secured.

Reaching the bottom floor Falau saw no response of any kind. He went to the dumbwaiter and opened the door, standing to the side. There sat Calvin, still unconscious in a crumpled heap.

Falau dragged his body and threw it into the back of the meat delivery truck. He smiled at the irony.

Stepping back into the kitchen he saw several towels lined up for the next day's work. He grabbed them and pushed one beneath his shirt to help stem the blood flowing from the knife wound in his shoulder.

Entering the van Falau kicked hard, breaking off the steering column and exposing the wires, allowing him to hotwire the car quickly and efficiently.

The car sprang to life and he put it into reverse, edging back, and then putting it into drive.

The small road was only a few hundred yards from the gate on the rear side of the property. Another road led to the main street up from the lake. The big man pushed hard down on the gas, bracing himself for the massive impact that the gate would have on the vehicle.

The van struck the gate at 80mph and smashed it clean off its hinges. Falau looked in the side mirror at the destruction. The gate wasn't reinforced like the front gate. It had probably been left more accessible for ease of use by the various delivery men.

Falau grabbed the cellphone from his pocket, wincing in pain. He flipped it open and called the predesignated number in the memory.

The phone was answered on the other end without a word.

"Done," said Falau.

"Text," replied a voice, and the line went dead

Moments later a text chimed through, saying Fenway Park.

Falau drove the van as casually and calmly as he could, considering the excitement raging through his body. He was close to the end but still vulnerable to anyone who may have been watching. The risk was high and all-consuming, just the way he liked it.

Pulling onto Yawkey Way next to Fenway Park, Falau saw a good-looking man walking along and slowed down. The man turned, showing himself. It was Tyler. The nightclubs were letting out in the area and the streets were filling with college kids who went out to enjoy themselves and to drink their fill of beer. They crowded the street making it impossible for the car to leave its spot along the curb.

Tyler placed his hand on the passenger side door and climbed in. "93 South."

Falau pulled out and did as he was instructed. No need to talk until Tyler made it clear it was okay. Falau had learned in his short time with Tyler that he was always being followed and listened to by the enemy.

Falau worked the van through the city and up onto 93 South just outside of China Town. He cruised for twenty minutes before Tyler finally lifted his hand, saying, "Here. Weymouth," and pointing to the exit.

Falau pulled off the ramp and started driving up a hill towards a set of lights. Tyler turned and smiled at Falau without saying a word. They were close. Tyler guided Falau through several rights and lefts that led them around the town along various routes. Finally they pulled into a restaurant.

"Go to the loading dock in the back. Then back the van into it. You know the drill."

The van bumped up against the loading dock and two men came from the door and opened the back of the van. They moved in and grabbed Calvin under the shoulders and dragged him into the restaurant without saying a word.

"Let's go," said Tyler, soon climbing the steps to the back of the restaurant.

"Sure thing," replied Falau, swiftly on his heels.

The dining room of the restaurant had been cleared and along the side wall sat nine judges dressed all in black and wearing black and white masks. They sat motionless and stared straight ahead.

Calvin had been placed in a chair along the opposite wall, his mouth still sewn shut.

Another man, overweight and reading through glasses that sat at the end of his large nose, moved the paper in his hand back and forth, trying to find the correct distance to make out the words.

Falau pulled in close to Tyler and leaned into his ear. "I have some evidence that could help this case out. There's more in the kid's room back at the house."

Falau pulled the pictures and prizes from his pocket and handed them to Tyler. He looked over and saw Calvin watching him with a look of rage as if Falau had just robbed him.

Falau tuned to see one of the judges observing his interaction with Tyler. The judge nodded, and Falau reciprocated.

The big man turned and walked out the back door, the same one he had entered through. Tyler followed, catching up to him on the loading dock.

"Hey. You're not going to stay for the trial?" questioned Falau.

"No. I know how this one will turn out. The evidence is overwhelming and without his daddy here to bail him out it's a done deal."

"You need some medical attention."

"I know. I got a guy for that. No questions asked. Oh, by the way... Calvin killed his father. The body is at the house."

"I know. We already have a team there taking care of things."

"I should have known,' said Falau, smiling. He walked down the loading dock stairs and started across the parking lot.

"Hey, Falau," called Tyler. "Nice touch with the sewing."

"It was the only way to shut that jerk up."

Chapter 37

The bell chimed its familiar chime as the door of the diner opened, letting in a gust of air. The seasons were changing and spring was on the way. Overcoats were getting less use and lighter hoodies and jackets were making their way into people's wardrobes.

Falau looked around the diner and saw Tyler's smiling face at the far end of the room. He sat in a booth with his back to the wall, just the way he always did. That seat was the position of power, the spot where you could take everything in and see who was coming and who was going. That spot also held a great view of the street down to the front door. Little was left to chance when it came to Tyler. He raised his hand and waved, ushering his friend to come sit with him at the booth.

Falau too was in a state of constant vigilance, his mind locked on everything happening around him. He had not had enough time to relax and let his guard down. Besides, his mind being occupied was not a bad thing. It kept the flashbacks at bay.

Sliding into the seat across from Tyler a large smile crossed his face, despite the grunt that came from deep inside him. The knife wound had still not fully healed, and he was refusing painkillers for fear he could get addicted, an acknowledgment of his drinking problem.

"That didn't sound good. You want to see my guy about that?" asked Tyler, a look of concern on his face.

"No, I'm good. Just the muscles working themselves out again. Slow going, but I'll be back to normal in a few weeks."

"Glad to hear it. Speaking of good news, did you get a chance to look at today's paper?"

"No, I'm afraid I don't get the paper where I live." The big man smiled, knowing full well how Tyler felt about where he lived.

Tyler slid a paper across the table. A banner headline extended above the fold of the paper, and just under the mast heading of the Boston Times, read;

Murder. Suicide. Evidence.

Falau read it. Beneath it was a large picture of Calvin Wise and his father from a golf outing they had years before.

Falau raised one eyebrow and looked at his friend. "Catchy headline."

"Yes. To the point. Seems that Calvin Wise really did kill those girls. There was a ton of evidence all over his bedroom. Even pictures of the girls and things that belonged to them."

Falau lifted his head, preferring to hear what the judges and the team had done from Tyler rather than reading it in the paper. "What a moron to leave that stuff sitting around."

"Guess he figured that daddy got him off the first time and that it wouldn't be a problem this time. But it was. From what the article says the father caught him and confronted him. The two got into a bloody fight and the kid killed the old man. Left his body just lying there on the bed. Then he went down and killed the guards working at the house."

Falau flashed a knowing smile, putting together why there had been no response from the guards as he fought with Calvin and removed him from the house. The sick killer had taken them out before he even got a chance to get to Calvin.

"Guess the kid couldn't take it," said Tyler, shaking his head in disgust. "The twisted prick zip-tied his own arms and legs, then tied a cinderblock from the garage to his feet. Pushed himself off the diving board and drowned himself."

"Wow. What a way to go."

"At least the families can have some peace now. The guy who killed their daughters is dead, just as he should be. Too bad he didn't just take himself out before all of this, and then the girls would not have died."

"What the hell is this world coming to,' asked Falau with a wry smile.

The big man knew that what Tyler was saying was right. They had done some good for the families of the girls who died. They finally had some justice. They would not have to see Calvin Wise's face smiling back at them from a picture in the newspaper, as he attended a swanky benefit while their daughters lay decomposing in a cold and lonely grave.

A buxom overweight waitress dressed in jeans and a t-shirt bumped up against the table. "That kid was one sick son of a bitch. Came in here once. Just had a weird look in his eyes. You want some lunch, hun?"

"Just a coffee and a corn muffin," Falau replied with a smile.

"Good," she replied, and turned and walked away, ending any possibility of chit-chat.

"Seems very cut and dry. No marks or other evidence in the house. What if another person was there," asked Falau, digging gently for information but being sure not to let others understand the true course of the conversation.

"I would doubt that. These guys are very thorough. If there were anything there they would have found it." A wink shot from Tyler's eye, catching Falau off guard. It was unlike his friend to make such a public display that could be picked up on.

"Oh, I almost forgot. I picked up that portable disk drive you wanted. Check it and make sure it's the right one. If not, I can bring it back," said Tyler as he reached below the table and pulled up a small bag, handing it across to Falau.

Falau accepted the bag willingly and opened it. He saw the box to the disk drive and opened the end. A stack of bills in twenty, fifty, and one-hundred-dollar denominations stared back at him as his flipped through them with his thumb. The stack was larger than he thought it would be. Smiling, he shut the box and placed the bag beside him as the corn muffin and coffee arrived.

The waitress made no attempt at conversation, as the two men looked up at her sliding the muffin in front of Falau and spilling the coffee as it clunked on the table. She turned and walked away without making eye contact.

"This city has the best waitresses," joked Falau, grabbing a napkin to wipe up the spilled coffee.

"The guy at the computer store put an extra ten gigs on that drive for you, because you had to wait so long to get it. He wants you to know he really appreciates your business."

Falau nodded his head, understanding that the extra $10,000 dollars on top of his fee was most likely payment for the time he'd spent in prison.

They have obviously never done time, or the number would be higher, thought Falau to himself, though he was not about to reject the money. He needed it badly. He was finally starting to get back on his feet after working with Tyler.

"If you talk to him again just let him know I love the work he does. If he stays open, I'd be happy to do business with him any time."

Tyler smiled at his friend and reached into his coat and pulled out a thick money clip stacked with twenty-dollar bills. He pulled one out and placed it on the table as he stood up.

"Coffee and the muffin is on me today. You pick up the next one. I'll give you a call."

Falau reached out his hand, grabbing the sleeve of Tyler's coat and looking up at him earnestly. "The other night in the van, you asked me if I really wanted this. Well, I've been thinking about it, and I do."

"I'm glad to hear that. I'm sure we can work together."

"You're not hearing me. I want this to be my life. It gives me purpose. Something real to believe in. I can do some good for a lot of people," whispered the big man without releasing his grip from his friend's sleeve.

Tyler looked down, examining his old friend.

Falau felt Tyler was assessing things, processing what level he wanted Falau to be at, what level of action he could take. Was he worth the time and effort, or was he okay doing just the work he was doing?

A smile curled Tyler's lips and he sat back down across the table from the big man.

"Do you realize what you're asking? This is very big. Life changing."

"I understand. I know there is more than what I do. I want that. I want to make a big impact."

Tyler's face hardened and his shoulders straightened. He leaned back and looked out the window, taking a short, audible breath. His head snapped back around to Falau and nodded up and down quickly. He leaned hard over the table, close to his friend.

"This isn't some summer camp. No part-time job. If you're in, you're in. You can't walk away from the next level. It's for life. And that's probably what it will cost you. Eventually, everyone gets taken out. Are you willing to take that chance?"

"Yes I am."

Tyler leaned back in the booth and let his eyes scan the room again, taking in every detail and wondering who might be there listening. The fingers on his right hand drummed the table in a few short bursts. "This goes against all my better judgment," he said, shaking his head. "But you always come through on the other side. You always get the job done. I will bring your application into the bosses and see what we can do."

"Thanks, man. You won't regret it."

"Yes, I will," said Tyler in a somber voice. The good-looking young man stood up from his seat, patted his friend on the shoulder, and walked out the door, the bell chiming as he left.

Don't miss out!

Click the button below and you can sign up to receive emails whenever Mike Gomes publishes a new book. There's no charge and no obligation.

https://books2read.com/r/B-A-DACE-DMGP

BOOKS 2 READ

Connecting independent readers to independent writers.

Also by Mike Gomes

The Young Adventurers' Club
The Fixer
The Young Adventurers Club Box Set
9 MM

Made in the USA
San Bernardino, CA
07 July 2019